STOWAWAY STAR RUNNER

C.G. HARRIS

Hot
Chocolate
Press

The Viraquin Voyage series is a 4-book space pirate adventure.
Think Guardians of the Galaxy meets Firefly

The Viraquin Voyage Completed Series:

Hometown Space Pirate

Stowaway Star Runner

Yuletide Space Ranger

Space Pirate Reunion

QR code for Free Novella, Fugitive Star Voyage,
to read the origin story for this series.

Join the C.G. Harris Legion

Join the C.G. Harris Legion to receive book intel, useless trivia, special
giveaways, plus you'll learn about Hula Harry and get his Drink of the Week.
https://www.cgharris.net/legion-sign-up-page

ONE

There are some things you just don't expect to find on your first trip into the cosmos. The secret to true happiness, a Starbucks drive through, a baby koala. As it turned out, the universe was full of surprises, and I found myself ill prepared to handle the very first one.

The world stopped spinning, and everything went still. Earth was no longer visible on the ship's front viewscreen and I looked over at Lois who stood to my right. Her eyes had gone as wide as mine as we did our best to rectify what had just occurred.

"Are you okay?" I did a quick check of all my own appendages and then examined the bridge. The icy blue walls, the touch screen panels and even our three captain's chairs seemed to be intact. "What happened and ... wait ... what is that smell? Is that your feet?"

I simultaneously pinched my nose closed, hiccuped and waved a hand in front of my face. "Come on. We're on a spaceship. It's not like we can roll down the windows and let in some fresh air."

"I believe the infant Lois is holding has folded us to another location in space." The new voice belonged to Buttercup, our space-faring battleship, and the not so artificial intelligent personality of its operating and navigation system. The name fit in the way you named a Rottweiler Fluffy. Too bad the irony seemed lost on her.

"The olfactory side effects and diaphragm spasms are likely a result of the fold as well. They should dissipate momentarily."

"My feet do not smell." Lois shuffled backward in her bright red pumps and let out a loud hiccup of her own.

Her yellow cardigan and plaid skirt were a contrast to her red-rimmed glasses and shoes, making a conservative, yet standout statement for someone with such a small stature. At least she made a statement. My six-foot four frame, black t-shirt and jeans said nothing except big, tall and boring.

She cradled the infant Viraquin in her arms. An adorable squid like baby that could have taken the Hallmark toy market by storm. It had tiny, stubby tentacles below an adorably fat body and a pudgy little face that would make the Grinch giggle with glee. A blue bioluminescent wave danced beneath its pink skin, matching its bright blue inquisitive eyes, and a tiny grin seemed perpetually poised to gurgle happy little noises in response to everything it saw.

Lois rocked the baby in her arms and sniffed, taking in a lung full of air as she turned her head from side to side. I crinkled my nose in disgust and tried to breathe through my mouth.

"I don't know what ... *hic* ... Ben's talking about." Lois sighed in ecstasy. "All I smell is hot apple pie."

"Ugh." I shook my head trying to escape the offensive odor. "Are you kidding me? I don't know ... *hic* ... what you put in your apple pies, but I am *never* eating one." I walked toward

Lois to check on our tiny passenger. "Do we have any idea where the mother went? Or where we are for that matter?"

"I know next to nothing about how the Viraquin folds through space." The sine wave that offered a visual representation of Buttercup's voice pulsed on the main viewscreen at the front of the bridge. "No one does. I don't even understand how this infant moved us here."

"So, we save the mom from the marauding robots, then she leaves us with her space folding baby bomb?" I ran my hand over my head with frustration.

The marauding robots in question were the Scavid; an artificially intelligent life form who wanted to harness the Viraquin's incredible ability to travel and use it as a weapon. We destroyed one of their ships to save the mother, but when they got wind of our new travel-sized companion, they would likely stop at nothing to obtain it.

"The mother had no choice," Lois defended. "She was dying. I'm sure she folded away in order to survive."

I patted the infant on its dome head, which caused it to flicker with bioluminescent light. "What about our ... *hic* ... location? Can you tell where we are? How far did we go?"

"Stand by."

Twitch, our resident mascot, glided in and landed on my shoulder, sniffing the air then huffing it out again as if he smelled something too. Twitch was a Chitterwall. An alien creature that resembled a cross between a flying squirrel and a red and blue macaw. He had beautiful plumage when he wasn't using his color-changing ability to camouflage himself against a background. He was intelligent and the best thief I had ever seen in my life. He also loved me and seemed less than thrilled about Lois, which as a biologist, left her more than a little frustrated.

"Navigational bearings are showing that we are somewhere in the ..."

She paused, raising my anxiety level from a twelve to a fifteen. "In the what? Don't tell me we're in some sort of enemy territory."

"We are not in enemy territory," Buttercup answered. "At least not so far as I can tell. We are actually in the Adlet system."

I looked at Lois. She shrugged at me, still rocking the baby Viraquin in her arms. "What is that, like a million miles from earth?"

"More like two hundred twelve trillion, give or take a few billion." Buttercup corrected. "The Adlet system is home to the Peeri."

I blinked in astonishment, not knowing how to respond to any of that.

Much to her credit, Lois turned her gaze toward the screen and smiled. "I know you're trying to help, but this is all new to us. Can you explain a little more?"

Buttercup groaned, making her visual sine wave reverberate with annoyance.

"The Peeri are what you refer to as Faeries."

I felt my eyes widen with recognition as I looked toward Lois. Her mouth fell open and we both peered at the baby Viraquin. Prior to our unscheduled departure from Earth's solar system, we discussed how to catch up to the baby's mother. Considering her unique proclivity to travel anywhere in the very large universe, it was hard to predict where she might have gone to heal and recover. Buttercup suggested we might visit a race of aliens who had a reputation for knowledge. A race Lois and I recognized as looking suspiciously like the fairies we were accustomed to seeing in movies and fantasy novels. That was when baby went all supernova, folding us to a strange galaxy and giving us the hiccups and smelly feet.

"Wait," I said. "None of this makes any sense. How did this baby even understand what we were talking about? It's a baby."

"I am unclear how, but the infant has somehow folded us across space, eliminating the considerable time it would have taken us to travel the same distance using my Warpstream drive."

I shook my head. "For the sake of conversation, I'm going to pretend I understand what a Warpstream thing is. More importantly are we saying this baby can fold us anywhere ... at any time?"

Lois lost some of her grin as the implications of that statement hit her.

We both looked at the baby and it erupted in a giggle that made us jump.

"Okay." I clapped my hands together. "First thing we need to do is avoid any stimulus that might cause it to warp ... fold or whatever."

"Her," Lois said.

I raised an eyebrow. "Excuse me?"

"She is a she, not an it."

"Annnnd how do you know that?"

"I am a biologist."

"And I'm a nurse. So what?"

She rolled her eyes as if that should be explanation enough. When I blinked at her, one eyebrow still cocked into the air, she went on.

"I studied Cephalopods most of my professional life. Granted she is an alien, but she has tiny little tentacles much like an octopus or a squid. A male cephalopod would have one arm called a hectocotylus which is used for reproduction and looks different than all the others. Hers are all the same so we can hypothesize she is a girl. At least until she gets old enough to tell us something else."

I gawked with my mouth half open not knowing what to say.

"You asked a question, and I gave you an answer."

I snapped my mouth shut and took a breath. "I stand corrected. We need to make sure we don't do anything that would cause *her*," I enunciated the pronoun for effect, "to fold into space again."

Lois nodded. "And we need to give her a name."

"What?"

"A name," She repeated. "We can't just keep calling her *She* all the time."

"Alright," I sighed. "We will give her a name ... later. Can we figure this whole space travel thing out first? I mean, if you don't mind."

Lois narrowed her eyes and glared at me but didn't say anything else.

"So, what did we do to make her fold to this location?" I said, ignoring her stare. "We mentioned ... F-A-I-R-I-E-S."

"I don't know if spelling out the word is going to make that much difference," Buttercup said. "The infant can't even speak."

Lois snickered then stopped as she caught my eye.

"What then?" I huffed "How did she know to come here?"

"I projected an image of the Peeri on the viewscreen before she folded us through space," Buttercup said. "Perhaps she intuited our intent somehow, though I am not sure how she could have known about the Peeri or the system they inhabit. Perhaps she perceived it through the Nexus."

"Okay," I said. "Pretend Lois and I are from Earth and have

no basis for anything you're talking about. Just act like we understand as much about space aliens as this baby ... actually, pretend we know less."

"I apologize," Buttercup said, but she still sounded annoyed. "Sometimes I forget you are both ignorant to many of the common terms I am familiar with."

"Ignorant seems like a strong word."

"Again, I apologize. How about oblivious, uneducated, nescient, green, birdbrained ..."

"Alright, you made your point." I held up my hand. "Just tell us about the Nexus."

"The Nexus is the term for the biological connection all advanced races have achieved with technology. The same way you connected with me. Most humans cannot do it ... not yet, but perhaps this infant can. She may have gained the information using a Nexus ability I am not familiar with."

"Maybe." I shook my head. "But wouldn't you know if she had connected with you? I mean it was a big production for me to do it. How could a baby make a connection without us knowing?"

"The Viraquin is a species no one knows much about." Lois cooed at the little baby. "Maybe it has abilities we aren't aware of."

"That is a frightening thought," I agreed. "She's full of enough surprises."

I peered at the little bundle wriggling in Lois's arms and saw bubbles streaming out if it's mouth. "Should you get a tissue or something?"

Lois broke out in a wide grin and looked up at me. "That's it."

"What's it?"

"Bubbles. Her name is Bubbles."

My face went slack in astonishment.

"It's a good name."

I shook my head. "You want to name her after drool."

"Bubbles." Lois insisted, her voice turning to that grinding tone she reserved only for arguments and disasters.

"Fine." I raised my hands. "Bubbles L. Drool it is."

Lois bared her teeth in a snarl to say something back, but Buttercup interrupted the conversation with an alarm.

"Incoming spacecraft. I am receiving a distress signal. It appears to be a stasis escape pod. The designator identifies it as a Peeri vessel. Shall we respond?"

TWO

"We have to help them." Lois stared at me as if her statement was the only possible answer.

"We don't even know who that is," I countered. "What if it's a serial killer jettisoned by the crew to get them off their ship? Or maybe they're infected with a terrible flesh-eating disease?"

"You're being ridiculous."

"Every alien in the universe will want to get their hands on this baby, and you want to pick up the first hitchhiker that happens along? I'm not the one being ridiculous. We need to protect little Bubbles here. We need to protect ourselves for that matter. We can't just take on every alien we see."

"Actually, we are required to respond to the distress call by law." Buttercup chimed in. "The A.S.S. mandates any ship within hailing distance must render aid if possible. We are the closest ship. I detect no other signatures in the area."

A.S.S. was the unfortunate acronym for the Allied Space Syndicate. The enforcement arm for law and order in the galaxy. I made it a point to mock the name every chance I got.

I groaned. "Does anyone see a big 'ol ass floating around out there? I know I don't. Who's going to know? We're in space." I waved my arms wide by way of example. "No one is going to see us. You said it is a stasis pod. Will the occupant survive until the next ship arrives?"

"That doesn't matter. We will know," Lois said. "How would you like it if someone left you out there in the frozen darkness?"

"If it were me, I wouldn't know any different because I'd be asleep in my own little stasis dreamland. So, I guess I'd be fine to wait for the next luxury ship full of supermodels to come along."

"Very funny." Lois rocked Bubbles in her arms and shook her head.

"I'm only trying to keep our little friend here safe." I tickled the smooth, warm dome of Bubble's head, eliciting another giggle and an array of bioluminescent light across her skin.

"Besides, we still don't understand what caused her to fold us here. What if she decides to jump again? We'll have a stranger on board and no way to get them home."

"There is one consideration you are both overlooking," Buttercup said. "Not only are we bound by law to rescue this pod, it also has a royal signature. As in, the occupant may have a royal lineage to the Peeri. If that is the case, the reward for rescuing such an individual could be significant."

"I feel like you should've led with that information." My eyes went to the floor as her words sunk in. We were a rogue ship with no funds or backing by any official government. I wasn't sure how things operated in space, but I would bet my life it wasn't free. Having some cash, or whatever aliens used, in our pockets couldn't hurt.

I turned and walked over to my captain's chair, resting my

hands on the back. Twitch rode faithfully on my shoulder as I stared at the icy blue walls that made up the majority of Buttercup's hull and the starry expanse of space displayed on the viewscreen.

"What are we talking about here, I mean how much money? What do space people use out here? I assume PayPal isn't a thing."

"I do not know what a Pay Pal is," Buttercup quipped. "But no, it is not a thing. Most elevated civilizations have adopted the galactic credit as a universal form of payment. However, this pod may be far more valuable."

I raised an eyebrow in curiosity. "Valuable how?"

Lois walked over to stand next to me, and Bubbles reached out with her tiny little tentacles. I looked into her big blue eyes and wanted to melt. How could a squid be so adorable?

"I think she wants you to hold her." Lois sounded giddy at the prospect, and she practically poured the alien infant into my arms before I had a chance to say no.

Bubbles wriggled and giggled in my grasp, making herself comfortable, then she peered up at me again, making little bubbles as her skin rippled with light.

"She likes you." Lois reached out and tickled the baby's head eliciting another giggle. Twitch ran down my arm from my shoulder to visit the new arrival as well.

"Bubbles is very cute." I nodded. "All the more reason we need to protect her, no matter how valuable this pod outside might be."

I tried to hand her back to Lois, but Bubbles let out a little grunt and pushed against me as if to say she had just gotten comfortable and was here to stay. I rolled my eyes and began to rock back and forth out of instinct.

"I know we're obligated to help this pod, but I don't think

it's worth the risk. Maybe we can hang back somewhere and monitor it to be sure nothing goes wrong until someone else comes along and—"

"Incoming warp signature. My sensors are picking up an approaching ship."

I smiled at Lois, partly out of relief and joy, but mostly because I was right.

"Problem solved. Someone else is here to respond to the call. We can retreat and let them retrieve the pod. The occupant will be saved, they will get the glory and Bubbles will stay safe and secret."

I looked at the viewscreen waiting for Buttercup to reverse her trajectory and back away from the stasis pod.

"Shouldn't we move away? Sort of, hang back and fly casual, but don't look like you're trying to fly casual."

Not a single glimmer of reaction from anyone. Space was going to be a boring place with no one to pick up on my Star Wars references.

"I believe another issue may have arisen that you should be aware of," Buttercup said.

I sighed. "What now?"

"I have intercepted the ship's broadcast designator. I am familiar with the captain of this vessel."

"Great," I said. "Give him a call and tell him the prize is all his. I don't understand the problem."

Buttercup paused for a moment. When she came back on, her voice had a tone that was full of malice and disgust.

"The captain of that ship is Olamer Rasalas. He is a black-market slave trader and gun runner. If he gets a hold of that pod, the occupants will not be returned to their home. They will be sold on the open market as a slave, or worse, tortured and ransomed for as many credits as Olamer can get."

THREE

I stared at the screen, peering at an image of an intimidating looking ship streaking into view. It was long, grey and menacing, bearing small rearward wings under a hulking fuselage. I could see gun ports lining the hull and small square openings that spoke suspiciously of torpedo tubes I had seen on submarines. The weapons on this ship might not be hot, but there was little doubt this guy had come ready for a fight.

I looked at Lois. She had her arms crossed and glared at me over the top of her red rimmed glasses. If Buttercup had eyes, I had a feeling she would be doing the same. This was not fair. How was a spaceship capable of laying on a guilt trip?

"Fine," I snapped at Buttercup. "What are our options?"

"We rescue the pod and destroy Olamer's ship with seismic missile charges."

When she didn't say anything else, I prompted, "Or ..."

"Or we destroy Olamer's ship with seismic missile charges then rescue the pod after Olamer is dead."

I looked at Lois. "Maybe we need an outside perspective here."

"We can always try to talk to him." She reached up and spun her own chair around and around in a circle as she considered. "He could be reasonable."

Buttercup scoffed. "Engaging weapons systems."

"No," I shouted, holding out a hand to stop her. "Lois is right. We should at least try to negotiate. If you engage weapons now, he'll assume we're looking for a fight."

"Obviously," Buttercup said, then sighed. "Weapons and shields on standby. Are you planning to wave that thing around on the screen while you are talking to him as well?"

It took me a moment to realize what she meant, then I looked at Bubbles cradled in my arm.

"She is not a thing, but you're right. We should keep her out of sight"

I set Bubbles down on my chair and spun it so the back was to the viewscreen. I swear she spit Buttercup a big raspberry before I turned her out of sight. She was only a few hours old, but somehow she seemed keenly aware of her surroundings. Something that should be impossible, but I supposed I would have to get used to seeing the impossible now that we were exploring the unknown expanses of space.

I stood next to my chair and Lois left her station to join me on the other side. Twitch hurried down to sit with Bubbles, but I wondered if that would be enough to keep her from wandering off.

"Do we have something to keep her busy for a few minutes?"

Lois thought about it for a second, then raised a finger in the air and hurried to her seat where she had stowed her purse of a thousand wonders. It was fire-engine red, the size of a briefcase and the only thing she managed to bring with us after our hasty exit from Earth. Somehow it always seemed to have exactly what we needed.

When she came back, Lois held a granola bar in her hand. I narrowed my eyes with skepticism.

"What?" She shrugged. "Who doesn't like granola bars?"

"How do we know Bubbles even eats granola? Maybe granola is poison to a baby Viraquin."

"Well unless you start lactating, we have to try something." Lois tore open the wrapper and broke the bar into tiny pieces before setting them onto the chair. "What are we going to do? Starve her to death?"

Twitch took the cue and retrieved a small piece from the seat, then offered it to Bubbles. She tasted it tentatively, then chewed and lit up with glee.

"See." Lois gloated. "She likes it."

"Yes, you are a genius biologist. Now can we talk to the nice space murderer?"

"Space slave trader," Buttercup corrected. "Though I have no doubt murder is within his purview."

"Excellent," I said. "Dial mister murdering slave trader and let's see if we can come to some sort of agreement. We're all bio-creatures sharing this universe, right? We should have something in common."

A video image of Olamer popped onto the screen and I jumped back a step.

"Holy Oculitis." I held up a finger. "Could you hold on one second please? Buttercup, can you mute the call?"

I spun around and took a moment to compose myself. Lois turned around to do the same.

"Woah," I shouted. "Buttercup, you have to warn us before you blast something like that onto the screen. You can't just hit us with a thing like that without some sort of preparation. Jeez. That was like a slap in the face."

"I can hear you."

The voice that came over the ship's speakers was deep and gravely like a badger that had eaten broken glass for breakfast.

"I am afraid there is no mute function on my communication array." Buttercup deadpanned. "I will work to resolve the issue for the future."

I turned around and faced the screen again, forcing myself to look at Olamer without flinching. I wasn't sure if Lois had managed the same, but I didn't want to glance over at her and make things worse than they already were.

"You do that." I nodded at the image on the screen. "Captain Olamer Rasalas, I presume."

The creature before me was not unfamiliar, though it was unexpected. He was huge and stocky with long unkempt hair and a beard braided with bones and beads. His face was dirty, and he wore metal bracers and armbands, but no shirt to cover his overly hairy torso. Several of his teeth were missing and most important of all, he had only one eye. I don't mean he was missing an eye ... he had one giant eyeball in the middle of his forehead. If a cyclops ever took up a career as a seventeenth century pirate, this is what it would look like, only more hunched and angry like a grizzly bear. And I wouldn't give odds to the bear in a fight.

"Please forgive my manners. I'm a bit new to this area and ..."

"Leave. The pod is mine."

I let out a curious laugh and tried not to lose my cool. "I understand you responded to the call as well, but we arrived here first so ..."

"Designation BT3RCP." Olamer interrupted again. "I know you are there. Where is your captain?"

I opened my mouth to bark a reply, but Buttercup cut me off before I could ruin my diplomatic demeanor.

"This is designation BT3RCP. I wish I could say it is good to see you."

Olamer let out a laugh, showing his sparse, yellowed teeth in a grin behind his filthy mustache and beard. "The feeling is mutual. Where is Captain Ferrick? Don't tell me the Scavid finally managed to scatter his ashes to the wind."

I could not help but tighten my lip in a sneer.

"Captain Ferrick, as well as the rest of my former crew, were lost against the Scavid." Buttercup tried to keep her tone even, but I could hear the pain and anger in her voice.

Olamer laughed again. "I always knew that old dog would die at the end of a laser. Too bad it was at the hand of the Scavid though. So, this is your new crew? I'm surprised you found a new captain considering your ... condition."

"Buttercup does not suffer from a condition." I broke in, finally having enough of Olamer's insults. "And I'm proud to be her captain."

That elicited another bout of laughter. I glanced over at the chair while I waited for Olamer to regain his composure and saw Twitch had his hand over Bubbles mouth. They both peered up at me with guilty eyes. Then Twitch pulled his arm back and Bubbles spit out the shiny green granola bar wrapper. I rolled my eyes and looked at Olamer.

"Stand down and relinquish your right to this pod according to galactic law. Retreat or we will take action to defend our claim."

I expected more laughter, but Olamer leaned into the

camera instead, peering at us with that big, brown, bulbous, bloodshot eye.

"Proud to be the captain of that ship? We will see how proud you and your first mate are when you're burning inside of it."

With that, the transmission went black. The view returned to a picture of Olamer's ship as he peeled off, coming around to an attack position. Alarms went off everywhere in our ship, and screens went red.

"Olamer has powered up weapons and is preparing to fire."

FOUR

A flash of bright green light on the screen blinded me and for a moment I thought Olamer had scored a hit. It was only when I saw huge bits of his hull exploding into space did I realize that Buttercup had fired her energy cannon.

I reached down and scooped Bubbles and Twitch into my hands and transferred them both into the rearward seat to my left then took my position in the captain's chair.

"How did you get a shot off that fast?" I said, watching Lois scramble into her seat as well. "I thought it took you some time to charge your weapons and bring up your shields."

"Correct," Buttercup said. "Your conversation with Olamer was not going well so while he hurled insults, I charged the energy cannon. I did so gradually so as not to alert his sensors. Your conversation gave me just enough time to bring them to full power. He did not have time to engage his shields."

Olamer returned fire but Buttercup was already moving. She spiraled down and around, maneuvering away from his cannons. I expected him to turn in behind us and give chase, but he didn't. Instead, he turned in the other direction, fired his thrusters in a bout of bright orange light and jetted away.

"Switching to Battlesight," Buttercup said, then the icy blue cave that made up the bridge disappeared leaving us with the very unnerving illusion of being suspended in the middle of an interstellar space battle. Our chairs, pertinent control and display screens were visible, but all around us were stars and deep black space. That and one red angry looking spaceship, burning its huge circular thrusters in an attempt to escape ... well, one engine anyway.

Olamer's ship, much larger than Buttercup, gained speed even though the port engine sputtered on and off, belching big clouds of black smoke.

"Where's he going?"

Lois pointed at a flashing red dot in the distance, and I could not believe we had all been so stupid.

"He's going for the pod!" she shouted. "We can't let him get there first."

Buttercup came around, but we were behind Olamer now. There was no way we could cut him off.

"Fire at him!" I pounded the arm of my chair. "Do something."

Lois reached up to engage her virtual weapons display, but Buttercup stopped her.

"At this angle a miss could overshoot and hit the stasis pod. Survival rate on an impact like that would be zero."

"We have to do something." I felt helpless. Here I was, sitting at the helm of a battleship and all I could do was watch Olamer limp casually toward his prize. "Can we get ahead of him?"

I knew the answer, but I had to ask anyway.

"Negative. Even with the disabled engine Olamer gained

too much of a head start. His engines are powerful. Though we are much more maneuverable, Olamer knew his strength and used it."

Buttercup growled out the words with frustration. "I do not like to admit it, but he is a shrewd tactician."

"Shrewd or not we have to outthink him," I said. "Come on. We only have a few seconds before he scoops that pod, then he'll be after us."

Lois scrolled through her weapons displays looking for anything that might work, then gasped.

"What about this?"

I looked at the translucent virtual screen in front of her face and smiled. "You're a genius. Fire. Buttercup, can you target the bow just above the bridge?"

"Way ahead of you, Captain."

Four orange streaks launched out of Buttercup's weapons bays and streaked toward Olamer's ship. We watched as they overtook the larger craft, then three connected, right on target. The fourth overshot, but it didn't matter. These weren't explosive warheads; they were rocket drones. A defensive weapon designed to disrupt and disorient, and in this case redirect.

Olamer's ship spun trying to shake the drones, but they held fast, and his maneuver only exaggerated the effect of the disruptive rockets as they began to fire at full burn. The thrust changed his trajectory, forcing the bow downward like a wrestler shoving his opponents head into the mat. The result was violent and immediate. Olamer curved off course at the last moment, leaving us a clear path to the pod.

"There it is." I scooted forward to the edge of my seat and pointed toward the tiny cigar shaped vessel floating in the darkness. Now that Olamer wasn't pursuing it, the metallic looking pod seemed almost serene. "Can you intercept before Olamer recovers?"

"Not a problem."

Buttercup never even had to alter her trajectory. She simply aligned herself with the floating pod, opened her cargo bay and let our new passenger float in. It was so seamless it felt almost too easy ... almost.

"Olamer is hailing us."

"Put him on screen."

"If you think having that pod will keep you safe, you are wrong." Olamer spit and shouted as he stormed around his bridge like an ogre. "I will destroy you, then pluck that pod out of the ruins. Your tricks won't save you this time."

I realized too late that Bubbles was exposed on the chair behind me, so I shot up to stand in front of her just as a very angry image of Olamer turned to stare at the screen.

"Look, there's no need for a fight. You win some and you lose some. Next time maybe you'll come out on top. No hard feelings."

Olamer hit a control panel, then a crash shook the ship, nearly knocking me off my feet. I staggered forward before Buttercup cut off the transmission, so I was out of position to hide Bubbles. I couldn't be sure, but I thought I saw Olamer glance at her before the transmission ended.

I cursed myself for being so careless, but it probably didn't matter. Even if Olamer did see her, it was only for a second, and he wouldn't know what he was looking at anyway. Right now, we had bigger problems.

Another crash shook the ship and Buttercup spiraled around and down trying to get away from Olamer's guns. It appeared our rocket drones had not been as effective as we thought. Olamer had shaken them off and managed to reposition his ship at our flank making it impossible for us to fire on him. We were ducks in a barrel and Olamer seemed determined to blast every last feather.

"Now might be a good time to show off that superior maneuverability you were bragging about earlier."

Another hit. This one blinked out the lights and electronics for a moment.

"Rear shields are at seventy percent and holding, but Olamer is in pursuit. Even with one engine disabled he has the advantage of position and firepower. At our maximum trajectory and speed, he will overtake us within moments. Olamer has outmaneuvered us twice. I am afraid he is going to make good on his promise. We cannot outrun his guns."

FIVE

"Can we just leave?" I shut my eyes for a moment as Buttercup pulled another of her spinning barrel roll maneuvers. The inertia dampeners prevented us from feeling much of the physical effects, but the visual cues from the spiraling stars and energy beams were enough to send my stomach into my throat.

"You must have some kind of Hyperdrive or super engine for traveling through space, right? What was that thing you mentioned earlier? Fire it up and let's go."

"The theory of a Hyperdrive was proven mathematically impossible centuries ago."

"Wait." Lois held up her hands. "Are you telling me we're out in the middle of space with no way to travel at hyperspace speeds? This is not acceptable. Why would you bring me out here? How can you be an interstellar spaceship with no means of interstellar travel?"

Lois had ramped up into that voice that could frighten predatory wildlife. She was on her feet, pumping her fists in angry panic. "There is a crazy one-eyed man back there trying to kill us. Now is not the time to tell us we are nothing but a fancy sardine can."

I looked at my crew mate, but she had her eyes fixed on the spot where Buttercup displayed her visual sine wave.

"Please calm yourself." Buttercup sounded strained and distracted. "I simply meant we do not have a Hyperdrive. Most modern space travel is accomplished using a Warpstream Generator. It does, however, require a great deal of energy and some time to power up before it can be engaged."

"And you didn't think this might be a good time to charge that thing up?" Now it was my turn to sound frustrated.

Buttercup spun again and dove hard, evading another barrage of energy fire.

"I am terribly sorry for the inconvenience, but I am somewhat busy keeping all of us alive. If you would like to take over manual flight controls ..."

The ship slowed with a purposeful jolt, and my eyes went wide with panic.

"No! I'm sorry. You're right. Keep spinning and dodging. Please don't stop."

Buttercup engaged her engines just in time to evade another shot.

"We're sorry." I looked over at Lois and she nodded in agreement. "We're just a little overwhelmed with the whole space-battle-death thing."

Buttercup didn't say anything for another moment, then finally responded.

"Apology accepted. However, I am not sure it is warranted. I am powering up our Warpstream drive, but at the rate Olamer is closing, we will run out of time. If he manages to get a missile lock, he will make good on his promise. I cannot take any aggressive action without exposing us to his attack. It is all I can do to evade his assault."

I glanced at Lois, but she was staring at Bubbles sitting in the opposite chair. I spun to peer at the cute little alien swishing and swaying on her seat. She gazed at the swirling stars with utter delight, giggling every time one of Olamer's energy bolts ripped by. It was all Twitch could do to keep her from running off after one.

Lois and I dove toward her at the same time. The sudden movement caused Bubbles to jump and even Twitch reared back in surprise. I worried Bubbles would start crying, or whatever it was a baby Viraquin did when they were frightened, so I held out my hand to calm her.

"It's okay sweetheart," I cooed. "We didn't mean to scare you. We were just wondering if you could do that space folding trick? It doesn't really matter where we go. Anywhere other than here. Can you do that?"

I raised my eyebrows and gave her a hopeful nod. She returned my expression with a gleeful giggle and no sign that she understood me whatsoever.

"Let me try," Lois tilted her head so Bubbles would shift her gaze to her. "Remember the Faeries? Do you remember bringing us here to where the Peeri live? The Peeri?" She raised her arms and made flapping motions as if she had wings. "Can you take us to see something else now?"

"Yeah," I said. "We want to go see something else fun. Do you know something fun? Like clowns or unicorns?"

"No!" Buttercup screamed over the ship's speakers making us all jump. "No unicorns. We would all die for sure. Focus on the Peeri."

Buttercup managed to overlay an image of the fairy-like creature she had showed before onto the front of the Battlesight display. Bubbles looked up and laughed and cooed. The feminine figure was long and lean, impeccably dressed in a dark robe and had dragonfly wings tucked against her back like an iridescent cape. I wasn't sure if Buttercup had brought up an image of the Peeri or Earth's version of a fairy. Either way, the figure was striking in its clarity.

"Yes." I tried to contain my urgency so as not to scare Bubbles. "Take us to them. Can you take us there?"

Lois and I both gestured and nodded at the image as we grinned like psychotic parents at their baby's first photo shoot.

Bubbles let out a long coo as she peered at the Peeri figure, then she fell over, landing on her back. She tossed and turned, giggling like mad, as if this were the most hilarious thing that had ever happened to her.

"Well at least she's going to die happy." I straightened and dropped my arms to my side as the obnoxious smile fell away from my face.

"Olamer has missile lock." Buttercup's voice was severe and determined, but I knew what those words meant. "I am shifting the railgun to attempt a countermeasure attack ... standby, incoming transmission."

"What?" I said. "Is Olamer calling to gloat? Tell him to screw himself. I assume a cyclops can do that."

"No," Buttercup said. "It is an Allied Space Syndicate Cruiser. They are inquiring about the distress call sent from the escape pod."

SIX

I turned to stare at Olamer's ship behind us in the virtual battle sight display, waiting for the missiles that would end our pilgrimage as space pirates. Moments passed and Buttercup held our course steady, but much to my surprise, nothing else happened.

"What's he waiting for?" Lois cried out so loud it made me flinch. I looked at Bubbles who had jerked a wide-eyed gaze in my direction as well, but Twitch laid a hand on her head to calm her.

"I believe the unexpected presence of the A.S.S. vessel has brought us to a standoff," Buttercup said. "By now they would have processed our broadcast designator signals as well as the one emanating from the pod. They will know who we are, or at least have a designator to trace if we should run."

I scowled at the screen. "That seems like more of a problem for both of us, not just Olamer. We aren't exactly flying on the grid here."

"It would be a problem if I was not using a counterfeit designator."

I grinned. "Nice. What about Olamer?"

"I am sure he is using a false designator as well. If we get caught, it would mean a great deal of trouble, but the point is, of course, not to get caught. Besides, we would have much larger problems to deal with if the A.S.S. managed to get their hands on us. So would Olamer."

"So, what now?" Lois said, staring at the screen as well. "If what you're saying is true, we can't fly into their lap."

"I would suggest opening a channel to Olamer to get a sense of where he stands. Perhaps we can negotiate a cease-fire. I have known Olamer for quite some time. He is rash and impulsive, but he has not survived this long by being stupid."

I glanced over at the chair where Twitch sat with Bubbles and made sure it was turned away from the screen this time.

"Keep our little friend quiet." I shot Twitch a wink and I swear he returned the gesture with a tiny thumbs up. Buttercup and I really needed to talk more about how much Twitch understood.

"Okay." I cleared my throat and put my arms down at my side, trying to take a neutral posture that looked neither threatening nor weak. "Go ahead and open the channel."

In less than a second Olamer appeared on a rectangular overlay on our Battlesight view, staring with that single bulging eye. His gaze went immediately to the chair where Bubbles sat, and my blood went cold. He had seen her after all. Did he know the true value of what we had on board? I tried to act like I hadn't noticed him staring at the back of her chair and cleared my throat.

"It seems like we have an uninvited guest to our party."

His eye came back to me, and his curious expression turned to an angry snarl.

"The A.S.S. is no concern of mine. Give me the pod and I will let you live."

"I believe the A.S.S. may be of great concern to you." Buttercup broke into the conversation and Olamer did nothing to hide his disgust at hearing her voice.

"What would they say if you destroyed the ship carrying the distress pod? The pod broadcasting a royal Peeri signature no less. You might get your shot off. You may even destroy this vessel, but could you dig through the wreckage in time to find your prize and get away?"

Olamer's eye went to the chair and it was all I could do to resist moving over to stand in his way.

"Maybe we should all wait here for the A.S.S. to arrive," I said. "I'm sure they can sort this out. You don't have anything to hide over there do you, Olamer? No reason to keep the A.S.S. away from that nice ship of yours?"

Olamer laughed. "You're bluffing. The A.S.S. would be just as interested in your ship as they would be in mine—perhaps more."

"Maybe," Lois said. "But of the two of us, you are the only one with an engine blown to bits. And how's your Warpstream whatchamacallit? I'll bet that's not looking so good either. Who do you think they'll catch first?"

I couldn't help but let the grin creep onto my lips as I watched Olamer face slowly turn red and boil over. I swear he didn't breathe for more than a minute.

"This is not over." He shouted at the screen, spit flying past his yellowed teeth and disgusting beard. "Space is much smaller than you think. We will meet again and when we do, we will finish this dance."

I nodded. "I'm not much of a dancer, but okay. You'll have to lead. I'm all left feet when ..."

The transmission ended and Olamer reduced speed, cutting off his pursuit. When his vessel turned, we all got a good look at the damage Buttercup did to his port side engine. It was all jagged, twisted metal and flying sparks. Part of me wondered if a mangled mess like that could be enough to destroy the whole ship. I was no expert, but it seemed like something that volatile had to be dangerous.

"We should consider retreating as well," Buttercup said. "Much as I would not like to admit it, Olamer is correct. We probably have more to lose than he does. If they impound this ship and discover I am a biological sentient who has been uploaded into a computer core, they would wipe my system and purge my memory."

"You mean they would kill you?" Lois said. "I can't believe they would do that. I thought they were supposed to be the good guys."

Buttercup was not just an AI construct; she was once a live sentient being. When she died, her lover uploaded her consciousness into this ship in order to save her. A process seen as highly illegal and unethical. When he died as her former captain, they finally parted, but Buttercup was left to live in exile in this ship.

"The A.S.S. enforces Galactic law. I am not only an illegal lifeform, I am also considered an abomination to most of the civilized universe."

I bared my teeth at the description I had asked her not to use anymore, but Buttercup cut me off before I could protest.

"I am not saying I agree with them, I am just stating a fact. Should we be caught, I would likely be obliterated, and you would not be better off. You are both unsanctioned lifeforms traveling without authorization. You would be detained or executed, then Bubbles would have no one except Twitch, since technically he is the only sanctioned alien on this ship."

Twitch looked at me and chittered.

"You really know how to paint a grim picture," I said.

"It is not grim. It is reality. Everyone has a weight around their ankle, life is about how you carry it. I am engaging Warp-stream. I plotted a random course away from the area. My cloak will shield our designator broadcast so the A.S.S. should not be able to follow. Enjoy the show."

We were still in Battlesight mode from our fight with Olamer, giving us a near 360-degree view of the surrounding space, so when the stars all around us turned to streaks of light, my jaw fell open in astonishment and wonder. A colored wave appeared across our bow as we traveled at speeds humanity only dreamed of in science fiction fantasies. Something that resembled the Aurora Borealis but in hues of red and gold. It was easily the most amazing and beautiful thing I had ever seen in my life, and we were watching it unfold all around us as if flying unfettered through space all by ourselves.

Bubbles let out a long slow trill. When I turned her chair around so she could see the colorful light cloud, she tottered from side to side with glee.

"This is absolutely incredible." Lois stared at the scene, eyes wide with awe. "I can't believe we're doing this. Last week I was in my lab, working on boring old Earth science. Now I'm in outer space. I mean it's crazy dangerous and we almost died, but this all makes it worthwhile don't you think?"

I marveled at the beauty all around me and hoped she was right. We took a big leap of faith on this journey and so far, things had only gone from bad to worse. This was pretty great though.

"I must admit, even I enjoy seeing the phenomenon of

Warpstream travel," Buttercup said. "Few things in this universe are as stunning or beautiful. With your permission, I will disengage Battlesight and revert power to our Warpstream engines."

I smiled and stared at the incredible light show. "Just a few more sec ..."

"Permission granted," Buttercup responded without waiting for an answer.

Our three-sixty view became opaque in a jolt of reality, returning us to the icy blue interior of Buttercup's cavernous looking bridge. We still had a view of the Warpstream on the front display screen, but it wasn't the same. The one-dimensional counterpart felt hollow and unimpressive compared to the immersive feeling of flight Battlesight provided.

"You know, when you ask for permission to do something, it's customary to wait for an answer before you decide to do it," I said, annoyed at being torn out of my utopia so abruptly.

"That would be inefficient when I am already aware of the proper response."

"You are missing the point of *asking* for permission."

Buttercup did one of her very computerish pauses as she processed my logic. "Perhaps you are correct. In the future I will allow you to finish your response before taking the appropriate action."

"Fine." I did not miss the insinuation that she would not do what I asked her to do. "I guess that's a start. Mind telling us where we're going?"

"I suggest we proceed along this navigational path long enough to elude any potential pursuers, then change course. There may be more survivors from the Peeri ship where the pod originated. We should trace its origin and check to see if anyone else needs assistance."

I put my head in my hands and groaned. "The last thing I want to do is let more creatures know about Bubbles' existence."

"Excuse me." Came a new voice from behind us. "I do not know who or what a Bubbles is, but you will leave the Peeri ship alone."

SEVEN

We all spun around to see an impeccably dressed figure standing behind us, just inside the door to the bridge. He wore a crisp, silk uniform of all black with several ribbons adorning the right breast. He was tall, at least as tall as me at six-foot four, but he had a slighter build, almost feminine, but not at all weak or fragile. His hair was forest green and trimmed to a perfect all-business cut that showed off his slender pointed ears. Most shocking was his skin. The ivory white color, set off his piercing blue eyes. Oh, and he had wings. Honest to goodness dragonfly wings, draped down his back like a prismatic cape to crown his exquisite appearance.

No one seemed to breathe for half a second, then Buttercup greeted him in a fashion I was all too familiar with.

The door behind him slammed shut with a bang, then a large circle on the ceiling irised open revealing Buttercup's defense arm. The robotic appendage jetted out of its dock so fast I feared she might impale our intruder's forehead with the barrel of the weapon attached to the end.

The Peeri never even flinched. He just stood as erect and proper as Batman's butler.

"I mean you no harm, nor do I offer any aggression toward you during this visit."

His professionalism seemed to draw Buttercup back a bit. I was a bit surprised when she withdrew her weapon from within one inch of his brain to a more civil three-foot distance.

"Who are you? How did you get out of your pod?" I paused then waved my hand as if erasing the questions. "Scratch that. What happened and why were you floating out here in space?"

The Peeri raised an eyebrow and clicked his teeth in obvious disapproval but said nothing else. Twitch hissed behind me and I turned to see him standing on the back of his chair. He changed from his usual red to a darker crimson, then shifted again to blend into the leather. I was relieved that the chair was still facing forward so the Peeri could not see Bubbles who remained concealed on the seat.

"Captain Roberts asked you a series of questions." Buttercup hedged her weapon forward a few inches. "I suggest you answer them."

The Peeri scanned the bridge as if seeing it for the first time. His eyes flicked from place to place looking both appalled and strangely impressed, sort of the way you might look at a teenager's bedroom.

"You have an artificial intelligence system for your ship. How quaint."

"Buttercup is not an artificial intelligence. And you are getting on my nerves." I glared at the Peeri, then realized I may have said too much when his quiet look of disdain turned to pure disgust.

"It is a bio-intelligence? By the gods, I would have been better off with the slave trader."

"How did you know about —?"

"It is customary to provide a guest with refreshments as well as returning his offer of non-aggression."

"Yeah, well I haven't made up my mind about that last part yet."

"Maybe we can all just take a step back here for a moment." Lois walked over to her purse and pulled out a tiny bottle of water. One of the plastic ones the size of a toddler's sippy cup. Then she smiled and made her way over to the Peeri.

"I apologize for my associates." Lois shot me a glare. "Please accept our offer of non-aggression and a small refreshment. I'm afraid it's all we have at the moment. You have caught us a bit off guard. Would you like to sit down?"

Lois motioned to her chair, and I simultaneously stepped back so I could spin Bubble's chair around as he moved, keeping her out of sight. I tried to keep it subtle, but a smoke grenade would have been less obvious.

He took the water bottle as if it had been dipped in Anthrax, holding it in two fingers as he glided gracefully toward the seat. He was about halfway there when his strength betrayed him. His knees buckled and he lost his proper bearing, almost toppling to the floor as he went.

Lois reached out to steady him and I surged forward to catch him as well. I went into E.R. mode out of reflex. Years of being a nurse had engrained certain automatic responses in me. I gripped his wrist searching for a pulse, looked into his eyes examining his pupils and observed his chest to see how he was breathing. It took me several seconds to realize I had no idea what I was looking for. This was an alien being. For all I knew he had three hearts and a set of gills on the back of his neck.

Buttercup had a more cynical response to his near collapse

and advanced her weapon, apparently suspecting some kind of trick.

"Could you get that thing out of our faces." I let go of the Peeri's wrist and waved her off, trying to get Buttercup to withdraw to a reasonable distance. "I don't think ... I'm sorry I didn't catch your name."

The Peeri took his seat and did his best to regain his erect stature. He probably would have stood again but I didn't think he had it in him to do so.

"I am Lintang Janus Izar, Prince of the Peeri and heir to the throne of planet Lillora. We must make haste to warn my people of an incredible danger. I am taking command of this ship in the name of the Peeri. Set course for Lillora. We have no time to lose."

EIGHT

"I hate to break this to you Lintang Izar, Prince of the Peeri."
I spit out each P with subtle condescension as I stood up
in front of him. "But you have zero authority on this ship. And
what danger? You haven't even told us why you were floating
around out here in that pod."

Lois straightened and took a step away once she saw he was
steady and so did I. It occurred to me that his near tumble had
drawn me away from the chair where Bubbles was hidden and
I hedged back in that direction as casually as I could, trying to
make it look like I wanted to lean on the chair.

"Disengaging Warpstream," Buttercup informed us. "I will
conceal our location inside this asteroid field while we interro-
gate the prisoner."

"He is not a prisoner." I kept my eyes on the Peeri while he
had his on me, no doubt sizing me up as well. "Not yet."

Lois let out a sigh. "You two are about as hospitable as a
Nazi war camp. We rescued this nice ... Peeri. He did not
attack us. Now both of you, be kind."

She ground out the last words in her serious tone that left absolutely no room for discussion.

"I'm sorry. Lois is right." I nodded and offered Prince Lintang a friendly smile. "You must have been through a lot. It's been a crazy week for us too. Why don't you start with how you got out here, Lin? May I call you Lin? Lintang Izar, Prince of the Peeri feels a bit formal. You can call me Ben. Lin and Ben. We could be a comedy team."

I offered my most winning smile.

Lin stared at me for a moment as if considering, then he looked over at Lois. "Are all humans this exhausting? I have never met one in person."

Lois coughed out a laugh. "This one more than most."

They both stared at me as if I were an anthropological exhibit.

"Why do I feel like you're always teaming up against me?" I glared at Lois.

"What else am I supposed to do, team up with you?" she scoffed. "That makes no sense."

"Can you just tell us why you were floating out there, all by yourself, in the middle of space?" I said, ending the conversation that would never go my way.

Lin nodded and fumbled with the water bottle in his hands. It took him a moment to work out the screw top, but once he did, he took a sip and spoke.

"My ship is a deep space exploration vessel. My people dedicate themselves to the survey and study of the unknown and undiscovered, both in familiar and unfamiliar areas of the universe. What I am about to tell you is considered a Peeri state secret, as it was a discovery made solely by my exploration vessel. We have direct and sole claim over the artifact, as well as any knowledge or information contained therein."

"Okay." I shrugged, laying my hand across the top of Bubbles' chair. I glanced down to see her and Twitch sitting quietly next to one another on the seat. If I didn't know better, I would think they were up to something, but I didn't have the time or opportunity to check. "None of this tells me why you were floating in space like a popsicle."

"I simply wanted to establish an understanding."

"Consider it established. Get to the popsicle part."

Lois shot me a glare and I shrugged and mouthed, *what?* in return. At this rate we would be ready for a geriatric home before he finished his story.

"During one of our deep space scans we located an anomaly we had not seen before." Lin continued. "When we investigated, we found an artifact of unknown origin."

"What kind of artifact?" I asked.

"It seems to be a species-built structure; however, it is nothing like we have ever encountered. Considering our rather immense information resources, finding something completely unknown is, to say the least, quite unusual."

"So, you jettisoned yourself out into space to try to get home and tell them about it." I rubbed the top of my head with my hand in frustration. "Your story isn't making any sense."

"Maybe if we exercise a little patience and self-control he will get to it." Lois pointed to the ground as if she were heeling her golden retriever.

I grumbled in response, but didn't say anything else.

Lin nodded and went on.

"Once we made contact with the artifact, we discovered several breaches in the outer casing. Teams attempted to infil-trate, but once they were inside, they found nothing. The space was empty. That was, however, when our difficulties began."

Lin took another sip of water then lowered the bottle to his lap, slowly twisting on the top with his long delicate fingers.

"The crew began to act strange. Making decisions and engaging in activities my people would find ... distasteful."

I raised an eyebrow. "Strange how? I don't mean to press, but considering we are in outer space dealing with an infinite number of alien species, the range of what might be considered distasteful could be pretty large."

Lin tightened his lips in a sneer of disgust and looked to the floor. "They were not acting like themselves, that should be enough."

I opened my mouth to say it was the polar opposite of enough, but Lois held up a hand to stay my objection. "And at what point did you use the escape pod? Were you forced to abandon your ship by the crew, or did you leave on your own?"

"If he was tasked with telling this story, I'd be surprised if they didn't make him walk the plank."

Lois shot me another glare and I cowed in response, not quite able to hide the grin on my face.

"The crew did not force me off my ship, however circumstances made it necessary for me to leave. Considering the strange behavioral changes exhibited by the crew, I decided to take action and prevent them from bringing the artifact to my home world, Lillora. I disabled the ship and jettisoned myself into space hoping to locate assistance."

"You stated that you disabled your ship." Buttercup broke into the conversation for the first time since introducing herself. She still held her defense arm at the ready, though it was high in the air and out of the way. "Please define any systems you left incapacitated."

That last word gave me pause. Having anything incapacitated on a ship when you were out in the dark expanse of space seemed like a very bad thing.

Lin raised his head in defiance and did not answer. It took me a second to realize he refused to acknowledge Buttercup because of who, or rather what she was, and my blood boiled with anger.

"Look, you might as well get over this little hang-up you have with Buttercup. She was as responsible for saving you as any of us were, maybe more. If you think you would fare better out there in your pod, I am happy to stuff you right back in and send you on your way."

Lin met my eyes for a moment then cleared his throat. "Perhaps I have been a bit harsh."

"Perhaps," I said, never wavering in my gaze. "Now, answer the question if you please."

"When I realized how severe and widespread the behavioral issues had become, I took it upon myself to disable the long-range communication systems and incapacitate the ship by removing the main power couplings."

I blinked at Lois, and she stared back at me. A missing power coupling and no comms sounded bad, but considering my nonexistent knowledge of spacecraft machinery, I had no real idea what that meant.

"Buttercup?" I questioned, hoping she would fill us in.

"Without the power couplings the ship will be severely disabled. It will have no propulsion capability and life support systems will be on auxiliary power only. With no long-range communications to call for help, once their backup power is exhausted, the crew will perish."

NINE

"Perish!" Lois shouted. "As in die? We have to help them."

I held up a finger and nodded toward the rear of the bridge, away from our new friend.

"Can I talk to you for just a minute?"

"Talk to me?" She scowled. "What's there to talk about? We need to hurry."

I stepped forward, grabbed her by the arm and pulled her away from our guest.

"We will just be a second. Buttercup, can you please keep an eye on him?"

"Of course." Her defense arm fidgeted as if to remind everyone, especially Lin, that it was still there.

Lois shuffled over behind me then yanked her arm out of my grip, more than a little annoyed. "What is your problem? We have to help those peopl ... Peeri."

I nodded. "I know, I know, but we do have this other problem." I whispered and eyed the chair where Bubbles sat obscured from Lin's view. "It's bad enough that we're risking this guy seeing her, what are we going to do with a whole ship full of Peeri peepers? And what if they're dangerous. Or worse, greedy. Did you notice how Lin seemed more interested in protecting his proprietary interest in that discovery than saving his own people? What if we get there and all they want to do is sell her off on the black market? We have to protect Bubbles. It's what we're out here to do."

Lois put her hands on her hips and stared at me. She had a way of making me feel small when she did that, even though I stood more than a foot and half taller than her.

"I want to protect Bubbles too, but when someone needs help, we can't just turn and look the other way. What if someone did that to us? What if we were the ones stranded out here? Wouldn't you want someone to come and help?"

I thought about it and raised a shoulder in indecision.

"Depends who's doing the saving. I mean if it were that Olamer guy ..."

"You're impossible."

"Look, I'm just saying we should find out more about the situation. Buttercup said they're on backup power. They probably have super space batteries or something. I'll bet they could last out here pretty much indefinitely."

"Buttercup." Lois turned her head slightly toward the screen. "Can you calculate how long the Peeri ship can last on auxiliary power?"

"Provided they were at full power when Prince Lintang disabled his ship, they could last approximately twenty-seven days."

"See twenty-seven. That's not bad." I lowered my voice, returning my attention to Lois, but she wasn't done.

"And can you tell from the information on the stasis pod when it was ejected from the ship?"

This took a moment longer. Lin sat, perfectly postured at

the edge of his chair staring at the viewscreen, acting as if he couldn't hear any of this.

"According to the onboard computer the pod was ejected twenty-five point three days ago."

I closed my eyes and pinched the bridge of my nose as Lois crossed her arms and stared up at me. She didn't say anything else. She didn't have to. Either we went after that ship, or they were going to die.

"Fine," I hissed through my teeth. I lowered my voice even more and leaned toward Lois to be sure Lin couldn't hear me. "But no one can see Bubbles. We have to keep her safe. Maybe we can keep her in my crew quarters somehow. We can take turns ..."

"Well, who do we have here?"

I jerked my head around to the side to see Twitch chittering like a maniac on the floor of the bridge. He had his arms out wide doing very little to conceal or impede the progress of a very curious looking baby Viraquin ambling along the deck behind him. Bubbles cooed and giggled as she used her tiny tentacles as legs to walk/waddle toward Lin. Somehow our Peeri visitor sat up even straighter than before. Then did something I had not seen him do from the first moment he arrived. Lin grinned.

I sprinted over and scooped Bubbles off the floor and placed her on the chair.

"That's none of your business," I growled. "And if you prefer to go on enjoying our hospitality, I suggest you wipe that predatory smile off your face before I do it for you."

Lois walked over and laid a hand on my arm. I hadn't realized just how ready I was to launch myself at Lin until Lois's gentle hand held me back.

"You misunderstand." Lin did not lose his grin, but now

that I wasn't feeling so defensive it looked less voracious. "You have some truly rare creatures aboard your vessel. First the Chitterwall." He motioned to Twitch who had scurried up my body and was now glaring at Lin from my shoulder. "Then that cute little creature comes out to say hello. May I assume it is an infant Viraquin? I have never witnessed a live specimen, frankly I don't know if anyone has, other than you. It is quite beautiful."

Lin rose from his chair with a visible effort but didn't make a move to walk any closer.

"May I see it?"

I glared at Lois, but she only shrugged. I supposed it was too late to hide anything now. Bubbles was out of the bag. At least we wouldn't have to worry about keeping her out of sight anymore.

I spun the chair around and our resident charmer swayed back and forth blowing little bubbles out of her mouth. Light coalesced over her skin and the bioluminescence became brighter and more erratic when she set her big blue eyes on us again.

"Astounding." Lin clasped his hands together in glee. "May I hold—"

I put an arm out stopping him from even finishing the sentence. "Don't push your luck. I haven't forgotten the fact that you doomed your entire crew out in space to a cold miserable death."

That was enough to wipe the smile off Lin's face. He nodded and retreated to his chair, seating himself on the edge as before.

"Quite right. My apologies. It does appear that I miscalculated my escape."

"Miscalculated?" Lois raised her eyebrows. "Forgetting to

carry the one on your income tax form is a miscalculation. This is mass murder."

"Hold on." I held out a hand. "I am not exactly a member of the Prince Lin fan club, but I don't think he meant to kill his crew—did you?"

"Of course not." Lin looked abashed. "My intentions were to escape and return to my home planet for help. I did not consider how many ships would pass me by without offering assistance despite galactic protocol to the contrary."

Lois shot me a sidelong glance, but I refused to acknowledge her.

"Alright," I said. "So, we plot a course to your ship, lend a hand and then we will be on our way."

"No." Lin stood, this time with more vigor. "I must be allowed to contact my home planet. They will send help. You have done quite enough."

I looked at Lois then to Bubbles, who sat on her chair looking cute and innocent as always.

"You won't be contacting anyone." I turned my voice cold and resolute. "No offense, but until we understand more about what's happening, I won't have you calling in Daddy's troops. The last thing we need is an armada of Peeri ships trying to cover up some royal incident. You may have good intentions, but I do not want to be a loose end when a bunch of Peeri warships arrive to sweep this trouble under the rug."

Worse, what if Lin really was interested in Bubbles. He could call in a whole fleet of ships to capture her. With that much firepower at his back there would be nothing we could do to stop him. Better he remained our *guest* until we could investigate.

"We'll go to your ship and see if we can render aid. After that, we'll figure out what we're going to do with you."

TEN

Dropping out of the Warpstream felt more like having an ocean tide settle you onto a beach than putting the brakes on in a car. It was not a screeching halt so much as the space around us just seemed to stop moving. It was a strange and unsettling feeling. I was also disappointed when the dazzling streaks of starlight on the display screen reverted back to a view of the vast darkness of space.

"Are we here?" I stood from my captain's chair and stretched. Lois and Lin both sat behind me in the copilot's seats, but Lois had Bubbles in her lap, sleeping soundly in the crook of her arm. Twitch, ever watchful, scurried down from the top of my chair to perch on my shoulder.

"We have arrived just outside of the desired coordinates," Buttercup answered. "Dropping out of the Warpstream in close proximity to the Peeri ship would not only be dangerous, we could elicit an unwanted reaction."

Lois gently scooted out from under her snoozing companion and stood to stare at the viewscreen with me.

"So, where's the ship? I don't see it."

"Standby."

Lois and I peered back to Lin who sat erect as ever in his chair. He stared at the slick blue hull as if unconcerned, but he looked every bit as relaxed as a wet cat.

"I have located the ship," Buttercup sounded satisfied and maybe a little excited. "Magnifying on screen."

The Peeri ship was, well exactly what a fairy spaceship should look like. It had an organic almond shape, but the hull was all crags and valleys as if it had been formed in a massive sandstorm rather than a factory. Iridescent color reflected off the surface, changing from greens to purples to pinks. It was large and altogether elegant and beautiful. Too bad Lin had rendered it a coffin for everyone inside.

"I implore you not to approach that vessel," Lin said, his eyes betraying worry for the first time. He stood with us, moving slow and deliberate so as not to trigger a defensive reaction from Buttercup though his wings vibrated with nervous tension. "The crew on that ship are unpredictable. There is no telling how they will react to your approach."

"What do you mean by unpredictable?" I asked. "Do you mean they will take an aggressive stance or just fly upside down or something?"

Lin shook his head. "Not aggressive. Just ... unpredictable."

I raised an eyebrow in obvious bewilderment and looked at Lois. She shook her head in confusion as well.

"If you are concerned about the actions of your crew," Buttercup chimed in, "connect with your vessel through the Nexus."

"Wait." I jerked my head around to face Lin, apprehension pricking the little hairs on the back of my neck. Twitch fluffed his plumage and hissed at Lin, responding to my alarm. "You can control your ship through the Nexus?"

"Not control," Buttercup amended. "But he would be aware of the crew's actions. The Peeri are more in tune with the Nexus than most species. While you and I enjoy a passive symbiotic relationship, the Peeri can use the Nexus for limited communication. They are consciously aware of their connections and can even extract information from the cosmos in a way no one else can. It is, in fact, the reason we traveled here to see them."

I waited for Lin to react. When he didn't, I prodded him further.

"So, you and your people are super spies?" I reached up and soothed Twitch, who seemed ready to attack at a moment's notice.

"We are not spies." He defended. "A spy would infiltrate and dig for secrets one is attempting to keep hidden. We simply collect information that is already available and disseminate it to those who might find it valuable or entertaining."

"So, you're the National Enquirer and TMZ all wrapped into one."

Lois snorted out a laugh. "Trust me, that is not better."

"I do not know of this enquiring TMZ, however if they disseminate useful information, I am sure they are an honorable entity."

I laughed. "They disseminate something, but honor is not it. So, can you do what Buttercup asked? Keep them from meeting us at the front door with a shotgun when we walk onto the property?"

Lin turned his head and looked away, crossing his arms in defiance.

I was about to engage in a more aggressive conversation about airlocks, and how long he could hold his breath, when Buttercup headed me off.

"We answered your call to rescue and save your life. We also returned you to your ship and crew. According to Peeri tradition this denotes an accord of promise. We have done you a favor and now you will do us one in return."

Lin huffed out a cynical laugh. "I will not have a bio-intelligence quoting Peeri custom to me. I could have survived indefinitely in that stasis pod, so technically you did not save my life. I did not wish to come back to my ship, so you have done me no favors here either. We have no accord and I owe you no obligation."

I peeled my lips back in a snarl and leaned closer to him, glaring at the side of his head.

"Be rude to Buttercup or anyone else on my crew one more time and you won't have to worry about a rescue." That drew a low growl from Twitch as well. I glared at Lin for another moment then turned my gaze to the viewscreen. "Besides, I'll bet the Peeri on that ship will be grateful to have their saboteur returned to face justice. We don't need to waste a favor on you. We are here for information, and something tells me your crew will be more than happy to deal when we turn you over to them."

Lin shrank a little and I knew I had hit a nerve. Maybe picking him up wouldn't be a total mistake after all. If returning him to his people could get us information about how or where to find Bubbles' mom, then it would all be worth it.

"So, what do we do now?" Lois asked. "Can we call them up on the screen or something? Maybe if they see we have the prince that will be enough."

"Prince Lintang?" Buttercup said, as if that should somehow answer the question.

When he continued to stare at the wall, Buttercup sighed and answered for him.

"According to Peeri custom, he is obligated to garner an introduction via the Nexus to ensure us safe passage. Even if we have not come to an accord agreement, we have offered no aggression or violence other than that necessary to ensure our safety. We have upheld proper etiquettes on our end, now it is his turn."

"Well?" I said. "What about it? Are you going to reach into the Nexus and say hello or do we have to dial them the old-fashioned way?"

Lin stood erect and impetuous a moment longer, then his posture failed in utter defeat.

"I cannot usher you an introduction through the Nexus. I am ashamed to say I was born with a genetic defect that left me lacking the gift to connect. Therefore, I cannot reach out to fulfill my part of the formality."

ELEVEN

Lois and I looked at him for a minute, before I coughed out a laugh that almost brought Bubbles out of her slumber on Lois's chair. Twitch stood on my shoulder mirroring my hands on hips position, and if I didn't know better, I would swear he was laughing right along with me.

Lois rounded on me to glare my laughter into silence again.

"What?" I said. "For all his talk about Humans and Buttercup being an inferior Bio-Intelligence, he's no better than we are."

"Maybe so, but that's no reason to act as childish as he does about it."

"If I may weigh in, I am on Ben's side," Buttercup said. "Our good prince has been nothing but insufferable since *we saved his life*." She annunciated the last words for effect. "I think he deserves a bit of scorn."

Lin held up his hand and stiffened his spine, bringing himself to his full slender stature once again.

"You are right. Perhaps I have earned your contempt. That notwithstanding, I must still ask that you do not make contact with that ship. Allow me to contact my people and have them deal with it in our own way. I am sure my father will repay you for your loyalty."

Lin did not sound at all sure about that last part. If anything, I got the feeling the word repay could be construed in a number of different contexts, and some of them weren't good. I still wasn't convinced big Daddy Lin wouldn't show up and wipe us off the map to *pay us back* for our good deed.

"Are you going to explain more about what's happening to your people over there?"

"I have described the conditions already. The crew have proven to be unpredictable in a way my people have never experienced before. It must be contained or ..."

Lin let the last part trail off and I wondered just how far he would actually go to make this anomaly go away. "Still pretty vague. I don't know about your planet, but on Earth, acting unpredictable is not grounds for an execution. Buttercup, do you know if they've detected us yet?"

"I have advanced to well within their sensor range. There is no doubt they know we are here. They have taken no defensive actions. No weapons or shields detected. Engines seem to be offline. I am sensing numerous lifeforms onboard. Life support must still be functioning."

"For now," Lois grumbled under her breath.

"Okay, Prince Lintang, heir to the throne of wherever. If you would be so kind to join us. You said you disabled long range communications. I assume this means short range transmissions are still possible?"

Lois and I lined up at the front of the bridge. Lin offered another of his curt nods, then joined us as well while Twitch remained stolidly on my shoulder.

"Buttercup, can you try to open a ... oh, wait a second."

I hurried back and turned Lois' chair so Bubbles faced the rear of the cabin, away from the screen. No point in advertising her presence to the crew. Not yet anyway.

I rejoined my team and narrowed my eyes at Lin in warning. "My little friend back there is our secret, understand? It would be unfortunate if anyone found out she was on this ship. Unfortunate for the person who told them, I mean. Is that clear enough for you?"

Lin nodded and turned toward the screen. "The Peeri are nothing if not good at keeping a secret."

"From the sounds of it, you are good at telling them too. Let's just be sure you stick to that first part."

Lin nodded again.

I looked to Lois and raised an eyebrow. "Ready?"

"Ready."

"Okay, Buttercup. Open a channel."

The view of the Peeri ship disappeared for a moment then a Peeri face appeared on screen. Her features were similar to Lin's: lean, pale and beautiful with stunning blue eyes. Her hair was stark white however and she wore something I had seldom seen on Lin. She had a broad gleaming smile.

"Well, hello there. I was wondering when you might call." The female Peeri chimed, her voice light and melodic. "Come on over. We are doing fine. It will be great to have some new visitors."

I couldn't see much of the background as the Peeri woman took up the majority of the screen, but what I could see looked bright and orderly. Well-lit walls and very little clutter. I had a feeling life on a Peeri ship was much less confined than Buttercup's constricted cabins.

Her eyes focused on Lin, and to my surprise she laughed with genuine cheer.

"Prince Lintang. We were all so worried about you after you left. I am glad you're safe. Please join us. The dock is prepped, and you are good for atmospheric coupling. See you soon."

She waggled her fingers in a wave then the screen went blank, showing nothing but the Peeri ship in space again.

"Like I said." Lin ground out the words with utter disgust. "Unpredictable, inexcusable."

I stared at him for a moment trying to figure out what he saw.

"Are you saying you sentenced them to death because," Lois screwed up her face in confusion as well. "They're being ... nice?"

"Of course not," Lin snapped. "You would not understand. You are not Peeri."

I shook my head. "Maybe you can enlighten us, because right now you look like a crazy old man who hoses down kids for playing on his lawn."

Lin clamped his mouth shut, seemingly content with the explanation he had already offered.

I looked at Lois and she looked at me, dumbfounded as to why anyone who seemed to possess a kind and courteous disposition should be sentenced to death.

"I might be able to offer some assistance here," Buttercup said. "I have had some interaction with the Peeri people, and they have a particular bearing or way of acting. They stand on ceremony and circumstance and do not believe in frivolity. The behavior of the Peeri in the transmission is counterintuitive to all I am accustomed to encountering with the Peeri people. Perhaps this is the anomaly Prince Lintang is referring to."

I looked over at Lin and raised my eyebrows for confirmation. He answered with a single curt nod.

I let out a laugh. "You are concerned because your crew got their proverbial sticks out of their butts? This keeps getting better and better. Thank goodness we didn't let you contact your king. They would have called in a nuclear strike on the Sesame Street gang."

I turned to Lois and nodded. "Just the same, we should probably take a few precautions. Buttercup, do you have anything in your bag of tricks in the cargo bay?"

I referred to a bank of locker like cubbies that I had yet to explore. I imagined they held untold artifacts and priceless objects from every corner of the universe. The mere prospect boggled the mind.

"Maybe we could find a few new toys to bring with us. I will want my revolver." A giddy worthy weapon straight out of a child's dream. It was futuristic, full of lights and could deal damage ranging from a stun, to a tank busting explosive. "And we should find something for Lois too. You have enough room in that purse of yours to hide a space bazooka."

Lois scoffed and started to say something, but I turned and headed toward the cargo hold, ushering her and Lin along with me. "Let's get geared up and ready to go. These new Peeri have better manners than our guest." I glanced back and eyed Lin for effect. "But if they are as unpredictable as our good prince believes they are, I want us to be ready for anything."

TWELVE

"Nothing?" I checked the selectable energy revolver I had holstered at my hip like an old west sidearm as we walked over to the airlock access at the far end of the cargo bay. Lin was with us, bringing up the rear, remaining just far enough behind to be impetuous and annoying. "There must be something Buttercup can give you. We have no idea what we're going to run into over there."

Lois raised her purse and patted it reverently on the side. "I have everything I could ever need right here."

"What, are you James Bond? Did Q fill your purse with exploding tissue and laser lipstick, or do you plan to defend yourself with water bottles and granola bars?"

She laughed. "Trust me, I have what I need."

"What about a small gun?" I pleaded. "Like the size of a cricket. You wouldn't even notice it was there."

"What am I going to do with a gun?" Lois scoffed. "I could never shoot anyone."

"You know you're the weapons officer," I quipped. "Since

we have known each other, you have shot at quite a few someones."

"That was different. They were shooting at us, and we were on a ship in space."

I blinked at her.

"You know what I mean." She let her purse hang at her side and brushed off her outfit, making sure everything was in place. I wondered momentarily if I should rethink my jeans and black t-shirt combo. It was far less impressive than Lois' coordinated ensemble.

I shrugged. "Okay. Just saying, better to have and not need and all that."

"Duly noted." She smiled and pressed the button to the airlock. The door swished open with a hiss of steam, and I smelled stale air and old oil.

I was about to step in when a doubt crept into my mind. "Maybe leaving Bubbles alone over here is a mistake." I scowled at Lois. "One of us should stay back. What if she wakes up while we're gone?"

Lois eyed me as she moved into the airlock with Lin. "She isn't alone. She has Twitch and Buttercup. Besides, we don't have any choice. You said it yourself. We can't risk exposing her to anyone else."

"True," I groaned, and moved in next to Lois. "It's bad enough that this guy knows." I jerked a thumb in Lin's direction, but he didn't so much as acknowledge it. He just stood there like an emotionless butler, always lurking too far away to be friendly.

"She's asleep," Lois said, trying to reassure me. "What's the worst thing that could happen?"

"She could have a complete meltdown and zap off with our

ship." I turned around ready to head back. "I'm not going. You meet the Peeri. I'm going to make sure our space folding baby doesn't hijack Buttercup."

Before I took a single step, the door leading out of our airlock slammed closed with a hiss.

"You are the captain of this vessel, so act like it," Buttercup chided over the intercom. "The Peeri expects to meet a delegation from this ship. As there are only two of you that means you are both going. I am a digitally enhanced biological intelligence capable of traversing the universe. I believe I am qualified to babysit an infant for a few minutes. Go do your job."

I let out a frustrated growl. She was right. Even if she wasn't, I was trapped and didn't have a choice. We were all going in there together whether I liked it or not.

I glanced at Lin standing just inside the airlock doors. He had his hands clasped at his waist looking more than a little unnerved despite his outward attempt to appear otherwise. At least I wasn't the only one unhappy about this little trip.

"Just so we're clear." I laid my hand on my revolver and his eyes went from my face to the butt of my gun. "Bubbles is to remain our little secret. We will all stay together, find out what's happening, and see what we can do to help. That's all. Agreed?"

Lois nodded next to me, but Lin just looked away. I figured that was about as much of an answer as I would get considering we were about to drag him back to the very ship he had abandoned several weeks ago.

"Good," I turned and faced the exit side of the airlock, reserved to the fact that we were going through with this visit. "Let's get this over with while we still have a ship to return to,"

"Acknowledged. Docking sequence is almost complete. I

will have audible communication with you once you are away. Lois, I took the liberty of installing a Translation Crawler in your ear while you napped earlier."

"You what?" Lois pawed both sides of her head as if she could wipe it off with her hands. "What do you mean installed? While I was sleeping? When was I sleeping?"

"Actually, I needed to install the crawler, so I induced unconsciousness with a microburst of gas near your olfactory sensor. Don't worry. No one noticed the drooling."

"No one noticed the what?" Lois glared at me for lack of anyone else to glare at. That and she probably didn't appreciate the smirk on my face.

"Like that's supposed to make it okay? You knocked me out and put some kind of ... bug in my ear?"

"Yes. I will be able to communicate with you when you are away from the ship as well as monitor your vital signs. You will also have direct and immediate access to a translation matrix that allows you to perceive and communicate in almost any language whether spoken or written."

Lois continued her glare as I grinned at her.

"Okay that is pretty cool," she admitted, "but no more installing things without my knowledge. Understand? That is not all right."

"Understood," Buttercup said.

We both turned to face the outer door and waited. After a moment of silence, I leaned toward her in a conspiratorial whisper. "If it makes you feel any better, she did the same thing to me, while I was unconscious, I mean. Well, she didn't knock me out, the Scavid did that. At least I think they did." I frowned, trying to remember the details.

"I don't want to talk about it." Lois continued to stare at the door. "If there's a bug crawling around in my head, I would rather pretend it's not there."

"Got it." I stood straight again. "No more brain bug talk. I won't even mention it again. Promise."

I waited a beat, then. "How do you think it got in there? Do you think it just crawled in through our ear or up through your nose or—"

The outer door began to hiss, and I felt my chest tighten with expectation. For all my sardonic distraction, I was nervous about what we might find on the other side of the door. Yes, the person we talked to seemed nice, but Lin was convinced something was wrong. Wrong enough that he sabotaged the ship and jettisoned himself into space. I don't care who you are, that is not a decision anyone took lightly.

I put a little steel into my spine and saw Lois do the same. Lin stepped forward to close the gap behind us, then the doors opened to reveal the outer dock and the Peeri ship. Their airlock was open as well and a delegation of Peeri waited for us on the other side.

The moment the door opened, they hurled handfuls of confetti in our direction. I was so surprised I nearly drew my revolver and stunned them all. Showers of tiny white paper floated through the air as music played and they blew makeshift horns that reminded me of plastic party favors on Earth. Not something they had on hand, but something they threw together at the last moment to make a crazy celebratory noise at our arrival.

We all stood dumbfounded. This was the crew Lin deemed unfit to return to his planet?

I turned to look at him and his face had gone slack with horror. Not some over-theatric surprise or shock, but the kind of true, unadulterated fear no one can fake.

"We should have let them die."

It was all he said before a stunning Peeri woman stepped forward and offered her hand in a warm greeting. I recognized her from our communication earlier. Long white hair, blue eyes and almost as tall as me.

"I am Captain Amalthea Eris Thalassa. Welcome to my ship. Please enter and be merry."

THIRTEEN

"Captain?" Lois said precisely what I was thinking. "I don't understand. I think we assumed Prince Lintang ..."

Captain Thalassa's eyes went to the Peeri standing behind us and she let out a laugh. It was not a demeaning or hurtful gesture, but rather a lighthearted acknowledgement of the misunderstanding.

"Prince. We are so glad to have you back. I hope you aren't still angry. I can tell you we bear no ill will for your actions. We are just happy you have returned safe to where you belong."

"I could never belong among a crew like this. You are a disgrace to all Peeri. How could you allow this to happen?"

Lin began to step forward, but I raised an arm to hold him off. "Easy big guy. Captain Thalassa was being friendly. Maybe you should try a little of the same."

For a moment I thought Lin might try to push past me. He was tall, but I outweighed him by at least half. Shoving his way through might be harder than he thinks. After a second, he took a step back, crossed his arms over his chest and looked away.

"All right then," I said. "Now that the formalities are taken care of, maybe you can give us a tour of the ship. Lin here tells me you have run into a few mechanical problems."

Captain Thalassa stepped forward and took Lois's hand. She grabbed mine as well then pulled us both forward, walking us through the procession of smiling Peeri lining their cargo hold.

"Please call me Alma. I am so happy to have you onboard my vessel. I would be honored to show you anything you like."

Everyone collapsed in on us as we entered, offering tactile greetings and hugs. It was like being away from family for years and then coming home again. The crew seemed genuinely happy to see us. Joyous music played through the speakers, and I could smell a sweet scent of pastries in the air. It was amazing, especially considering the trepidation Lin expressed before our arrival.

"Would you like to dance?" A Peeri woman grabbed my hand and tried to pull me away from our little group. A few of the others clapped with encouragement, and though I was not a dancer I had to admit I was tempted. The environment was intoxicating. The smells, the Peeri, the music. It was all so ... happy.

"Ben ... Troub ... Comm ..." The voice broke into my head, making me jump with surprise. It was Buttercup, but the transmission was all broken up.

"Are you getting that?" Lois looked at me, smiling, but I could tell it was a strained facsimile of the real thing. "Buttercup is trying to reach you. Can you hear her?"

"I shook my head and smiled back. "I'm sure she's fine. This place is amazing, isn't it? We should stay for a while."

My eyes flicked from Peeri to Peeri as they danced and laughed. Unlike Lin, they all held their beautiful wings aloft as if proud to display them to the world. I caught more than one friendly eye as they touched and caressed one another. In the corner I saw ... woah. I turned my head and blushed. These Peeri really knew how to party.

"We can have fun too." A Peeri woman giggled in my ear. She caught my embarrassed reaction. "Come and dance. There will be plenty of time for duty later."

She was tall and slender and beautiful. Her wings fluttered softly at her sides as she gave me a seductive look and pulled at my arm. I found myself powerless to resist her.

"Maybe just one dance." I turned my head to speak to Lois and Lin over my shoulder, but my eyes never left the Peeri tugging me forward.

"What?" I had a sense of something pulling at my shirt, but I ignored it. "Where are you going? You can't ..."

The rest of Lois's words were lost in the glorious music and the sight of the beautiful Peeri woman beginning to dance before me.

Was our mission here really all that important? We had plenty of time. What good was it to travel the universe if we didn't take a moment to enjoy it, right? I stepped forward, pulling the Peeri woman close, losing myself in her sultry movements. That's when Buttercup kicked in the door to my brain and brought the world crashing in again.

"Ben, can you hear me? I have been experiencing some interference on our channel, but I believe I have cleared it up. Are you reading me?"

I shook my head and looked around feeling as if someone had thrown a bucket of ice water in my face ... then hit me with the bucket too. Lois and Lin stood to my left, staring at me as if I had grown a third eye on my forehead. Alma remained just past them, looking out upon her crew with glee and reverence as she swayed back and forth to the cheerful music.

"What is wrong with you?" Lois grabbed my shirt and spun me around. Her voice had turned to that gravely serious tone. "We do not have time for this. Get your head straight. We are here to help them fix their ship, not party and ... do whatever it is you are doing."

She let go of my shirt and glared into my eyes, all but daring me to move my hips one more time.

"I can hear you," I said, answering Buttercup. "Sorry. I'm not sure what happened there. Maybe the hull was blocking the transmission or something."

"It was more than that." Buttercup's frantic voice sounded relieved the moment I answered. "The problem was also interfering with our Nexus connection. Our neural link was down for several seconds. It did not damage any of the onboard systems but proceed with caution. I will monitor communications and the Nexus. If the anomalies continue, I suggest we retreat until I can investigate it further."

"Understood."

Buttercup was right. I had been so caught up in Alma and her welcome committee I almost forgot why we were here. More than that. I didn't care. Did the Peeri exude a hormone that could scramble my brain? Something in my limited folklore vocabulary seemed to think so. I would have to check it out when I got back to the ship. Until then I needed to be more cautious about controlling my emotions.

I looked at Lois who continued to stare at me. I mouthed the word *sorry*, then tapped Alma on the shoulder.

"Do you think you could show us to the section where you're having engine problems? We are in a bit of a hurry and need to get back to our ship."

Alma looked over at the three of us and smiled as if we had just arrived all over again.

"Hello. Yes. Of course. I'll bet Lin knows the way better than all of us." She chuckled.

I laughed but I had to force it. After all she was talking about the fact that Lin had tried to kill her along with the entire crew, and she was joking about it.

"So, Lin tells me you found some sort of artifact out in deep space. I didn't see it when we arrived. Do you still have it?"

Alma opened the door to a passageway and led us forward. The walls reminded me of bright white marble with purple and green iridescent stripes that ran the entire length of the hall. Doors and delicate view screens made of a material that resembled dragonfly wings dotted the corridor as we walked, making the place look like a formal receiving area for fanciful royalty.

Most of the crew must have been in the cargo section to receive us because the halls were empty. Not a single Peeri passed us as we navigated to our destination.

"Yes. We would never allow such a wonderful gift to be lost."

Alma stopped at one of the display screens and pressed her palm to the surface. Her wings had smoothed down her back like a shimmering cape similar to Lin's, making it easier for all of us to walk and move close to one another. The colors on the screen shimmered for a moment then an external view of the ship appeared. I could see Buttercup attached to their airlock on the starboard side then as the view shifted, something else came into view on the port.

The rough-cut cube was much smaller than I expected and was almost fully concealed by the bulk of the Peeri ship. It was even smaller than Buttercup by half and looked as if it had been chiseled out of a block of pure obsidian. There were jagged edges, rough gouges and long cracks everywhere, but as I examined it closer, I began to realize these were not accidents, but purposeful architectural aspects of the cube.

This was not some random rock chiseled out of a mountain, this was an exquisite sample of technology, built piece by piece into a strange black geodesic structure that boggled the mind.

"Wow," Lois said. "That is ..."

"Weird." I finished for her."

"But cool."

Alma laughed. "Yes. Weird, cool and beautiful. My people have never encountered an object like it. Once I bring this to Lillora, the Peeri will be forever changed." She spread her arms wide, her wings fluttered, and she threw her head back as if in ecstasy.

"You cannot do this." Lin stepped forward. I still saw the anger on his face, but it was more controlled now. "You must not destroy all we have worked centuries to achieve."

Alma brought her arms forward and cupped his face in her palms in a gesture of complete caring and serenity.

"My dear, sweet, Prince. Why can't you see? Our people live in darkness and anger. The Peeri are a joyless species. We have achieved nothing but greed and solemn isolation. This ..."

She gestured to the cube displayed on the screen and smiled.

"This will change everything. An artifact that will become our fountain of youth. This will bring us new joy, new life. A way of thinking we have lost. This is our future, and our future is happiness."

Alma leaned forward and tried to kiss the prince, but Lin pulled away in disgust.

"This is not salvation, this is heresy."

I laughed. "Heresy might be a little harsh," I said "But there is nothing wrong with letting off a little steam. I think whatever's on that cube might be earth's equivalent to good old Mary Jane."

Lois looked at me and cocked her head to the side.

"They're all high. Can't you see? They're just having a good time. The only thing I can't figure is why Prince Stuffed Shirt here isn't affected."

Lin curled his lip in a sneer of disgust. "I felt a momentary reaction to the artifact, but I would not allow myself to succumb to its effects."

I laughed. "You can't choose whether or not to feel the effects of a drug ... if that's what this is. Though if there were one being in the universe stiff enough to resist getting high and letting off a little steam, it would be you."

"The Peeri do not let off steam. We are a dignified and proper race, and this sort of debauchery is inexcusable."

I raised my hand to him by way of example. "See what I mean."

Lois let out a chuckle then covered her mouth before any more laughter could escape. "Maybe you're right, but how is it getting in and why aren't we affected?"

I shrugged. "Something about our biochemical makeup, I guess. We should be more careful about these little visits in the future. Whatever this is could have killed us just as easily."

That sobering thought was enough to bring Lois up short. "What if it's still here? Are we breathing it now?"

Alma spread her arms wide. "Of course. It is all among us. This is what I wanted to share. Come. Enjoy the happiness and breathe in the gift of the cube."

FOURTEEN

"We have to get out of here." Lois reached into her purse and retrieved a familiar red and blue floral silk scarf and held it to her nose. She tried to retain a carefree expression, but she was beginning to look a little panicked. I had connected the dots a little faster but didn't feel much better than she did about being in an atmosphere with something we could not see, smell, or understand. This might be the equivalent of an innocent high for the Peeri, but there was no way of knowing what the long-term effects could be to humans. If the *cube gift* was already in our bloodstream, we might never be able to get rid of it.

"I know." I put a gentle hand on her arm and lowered the scarf from her face. "But we're here, and there is nothing we can do about it now. Let's see if we can get what we came for."

Lois nodded, but I saw the uneasiness on her face.

I wasn't *just* interested in saving this ship. We needed information, and if Buttercup was right, we needed a way to barter for it.

I looked to Alma and smiled. "Why don't you show us to that engine trouble?"

Alma looked to Lin, and he looked to the floor. "I had every intention of returning in time to save you. I never wanted you to perish, though seeing you in this state makes me wonder if I should have scuttled the ship while I was still here. You cannot believe you are doing the right thing by bringing this cube to Lillora."

I clasped a hand onto Lin's shoulder and the other onto Alma's. "Maybe we should stick to saving lives rather than question whether we should or should not have committed mass murder."

Lin frowned, but Alma only laughed. "Right this way."

She led us around a few more turns then through another of the automated dragonfly doors. Inside was a room that resembled something more like a futuristic computer server than a power plant for a spacecraft.

"I assume Lin had his fun in here somewhere." Alma raised her hands and motioned at the flashing lights, glowing translucent cases and industrial looking connections that surrounded us. "Though we have not taken the time to figure out precisely where."

"Wait." Lois had tucked her scarf away and had her purse under her arm again. "You knew that you were going to die, and you haven't even bothered to try and fix it? You don't even know what's wrong?"

Even I had to admit that was a little on the extreme side of the joy button. Being happy is one thing, but what good is it to be happy when you're dead.

"We live in the moment. We understand the consequences and know our time could be short, so we are making the best of a bad situation."

"Well." I nodded. "I guess that's one way to look at it."

I turned my attention to Lin and motioned to the room. "So, are you going to tell us exactly what you did to disable the ship, or do we have to look around and guess?"

Lin stood for a moment, glowering at me, then sighed. "I've already told you. I removed the main power couplings and jettisoned them from the airlock. It is an easy repair ... if you have the correct components."

"Great," I said. "Sort of like pulling out the car keys and throwing them into the field. All we have to do is find them ... it ... whatever they are."

"Do you typically melt these car keys to slag before throwing them into the field?" Lin deadpanned.

I blinked.

"Okay, new plan. We can take someone from your ship to your planet and they can bring help. I would take Lin, but I think the only help he would bring is the exploding kind."

Alma shook her head. "We would not survive long enough for a one-way trip, much less long enough to go both ways. Even if we used your communicator to contact our planet, they would not be able to send an envoy to save us before our power was depleted."

"This is crazy," Lois said. "There has to be a way to make this work. We're not just going to let you all die."

"Without the proper parts we cannot survive."

"Then we'll just have to get the parts." I looked from Lois to Alma and back again. "What? We just need to find someone who has these couplings. How hard can it be, right? We go get the parts, bring them back and Bob's your uncle. You're in business and you owe us a favor."

I set my eyes on Alma and for the first time the room seemed to go still. Lin had his wits about him so I figured he would catch on quickly, but I didn't expect the fun-loving Alma to zone in on the bargain quite so fast. They really did take this tit-for-tat thing seriously.

"And what would you ask in return?"

"We need information."

"General information or would you like to know about something more specific?"

Alma's stare was almost hypnotic, and I got the feeling that the only thing more intoxicating to the Peeri than the cube might be the art of the deal.

"We need to know something pretty specific, but the nature of the information is ... sensitive." I glanced over at Lin and saw that he was staring at us intently as well. His mouth was clamped shut in a tight line that told me he wanted to say something, but he dared not interrupt.

"It will be difficult to provide an answer when I do not know the question."

I sighed. This was something I had considered but didn't know how to solve. I could not reveal our interest in the Viraquin without jeopardizing Bubbles. The Peeri had an ear out for anything. The moment they got word that a baby Viraquin was on the loose, Alma would be able to deduce just where to find it.

I was about to craft a carefully worded response when Buttercup broke into my brain comm.

"It's happening again! Bubbles is awake and she is not happy. She is folding and I have no idea where she is going!"

FIFTEEN

"**B**uttercup." I shouted, half crouched, not sure if I should run, stand still or do a little of both. "What's happening? What—"

A light bloomed before me out of thin air. We all stared at it in wonder, even though Lois and I had seen it before. Space seemed to warp around the point of light, bending inward like a dimpled balloon, then out popped Bubbles and space popped back into shape with her.

Lois and I lurched forward to catch the falling Viraquin infant as it cooed and giggled in the air. Our hands met beneath her and so did our skulls. We managed to maintain our position despite the catastrophic thunk, and Bubbles settled safely into our hands before she hit the floor.

"That was extraordinary." Lin stared at Bubbles with wide-eyed fascination that was not quite glee, but not at all greed or envy. More awe and amazement. "Does that happen often?"

Lois and I straightened, and I pulled Bubbles in close as Lois let go with both of her hands to rub her head.

"We're pretty new to this." I reached up with one of my

own hands and rubbed the spot where Lois and I connected, feeling a large welt rising on my skull. "I think this must be like a teething phase."

Alma let out a laugh that made us all jump with surprise. All of us except Bubbles. She just laughed in return.

"She is gone. Bubbles is gone! Do you read?" Buttercup's voice was frantic, and I would have given her a hard time if her concern weren't so genuine.

"Bubbles is with us," I said. "Somehow she found us and folded here."

"Oh, thank the stars," Buttercup sighed. "I had no idea how I was going to track a baby Viraquin through space. Tell Bubbles, Buttercup is very upset with her."

I could not help but snicker. "I will tell her, I promise."

Alma reached out and touched Bubbles' bioluminescent head and smiled at her before I could pull away. She didn't seem malicious or envious at all. Either the *cube* gift was doing its job or Bubbles was just too darn cute to covet.

"I think anyone would be new to this. No one has seen a baby Viraquin in ... well I don't know if anyone has ever seen one. And that is saying something considering the substantial information resources I have at my disposal. I only know of them myself through myths and legends."

I sighed and looked at Bubbles. "You're not going to make this easy are you."

Bubbles giggled, peered back up at me and cooed.

"Well, I suppose you know the nature of our question now." I looked to Alma again, doing my best to resume our serious tone, though it was much harder with a baby Viraquin in my arms. "We want to return her to her mother. We need to know if there is a place where a Viraquin might go to ..."

I held off saying the word heal.

"Get back to their roots. Maybe a home world or a place where they could rest and recover."

"There is such a place." Alma's face was no longer serious but rather joyful and happy. "If you bring me the part, I will provide the information you require."

"Dea—" I started to say, but Lois broke in and cut me off. "What if we can't? What if we can't get the parts, but we risk our lives trying to get them?"

"Then you earn nothing." She smiled and began to dance around the room to a new song lulling through the ship's speakers. "We will die, and you will never find your sweet infant's mother."

My mouth turned down in a scowl. "What if we just leave here and head to your planet? Make a deal with them directly. We could offer this cube in exchange. You won't make it but ..."

Alma laughed again. "No one on Lillora will bargain with two rogue humans and an abomination. You are fortunate to have come to me. If it had not been for the enlightenment of the cube, I would have destroyed your ship outright." She giggled again.

I looked to Lin.

"She is correct," he confirmed. "My people do not take kindly to those who do not conform to our standards."

"And he would know." Alma continued in a singsong voice. "The son of a king and here he is, a reject outcast on a deep space mission to nowhere. They would not even give him a commission. Only a consultant. Isn't that sad. That is the true gift of the cube. It will allow us to transcend all of that. I don't care that you do not fit a royal standard or that you are from a fledgling planet. I don't even care about the bio-intelligence system on your ship. I only care about joy and peace and love.

Bring me those parts and help me to spread this gift to my people."

I looked to Lois then Lin. Lin shook his head in a slow but self-assured no. Then Bubbles drew my attention with another coo. How could anyone seeking happiness and peace be bad?

"One other thing." I brought my eyes up to Alma again, fixing my gaze on her. "Forget you ever saw our little friend here. Anyone asks about the Viraquin baby, the mother, or even the legend surrounding the Viraquin and you have never heard of us. Most importantly, you never saw her."

Alma's jovial blue eyes went to the adorable bioluminescent bundle squirming in my arm.

"That is a valuable piece of information. Maybe too valuable to withhold for free."

"How valuable are your lives? How much is this cube really worth to your people? Isn't bringing it to them worth keeping one tiny secret?"

Alma continued to smile at Bubbles, considering my words then nodded. "I agree. Knowledge of this exquisite creature is precious but not so precious as the future of my people. Bring my coupling and make it possible for me to return and your secret will never leave my lips."

"Deal," I said. "We will bring your parts. Just be sure you're able to hold up the rest of the bargain too. One last question. How are we going to know what parts we need? I am not exactly a Peeri space mechanic. I might need a photo or something."

"That's easy." Alma pointed at Lin. "You will have a resident expert. Prince Lintang is going with you."

SIXTEEN

"Captain, I must protest." Lin repeated the statement for the sixth time, but who's counting. "I see no reason for me to accompany these ..." He cast Lois and I a sidelong glance then lowered his voice to a whisper we could still hear. "Their ship is a bio-intelligence."

Alma smiled and let out a little laugh as we wandered back through the cargo hold of her ship. The Peeri party had really kicked up a notch since we left. Confetti littered the floor, there were overturned crates and boxes everywhere and the music had ramped up from cheery festival tunes to Saturday night rave. The crew writhed and danced in time to the beat, bumping and grinding all of us as we tried to make our way through to the airlock on the other side.

I did my best to keep Bubbles hidden. Lois had pulled a red and yellow floral scarf out of her bag, and I draped it over my arm to veil her from view. Fortunately, the Peeri didn't find it unusual for a six-foot four man to carry a flowery scarf as an adornment. Less fortunate was Bubbles reaction to the music. She began to flash and sway her bioluminescent light to the beat in a visually hypnotic dance of her own. The eerie blue glow shone straight through the thin floral scarf like a manic lava lamp gurgling in time to the music.

"Wow." A male Peeri with green hair and no shirt reached out to touch the bundle in my arm. "So beautif—"

I smacked his hand hard and raised a finger. "Hands to yourself buddy. No means no."

We managed to weave our way through the partying Peeri crew members and get to the airlock on the far side.

"Consider this your penance," Alma said, apparently continuing the conversation with Lin. I had missed most of it as we navigated through the gyrating crowd, but now that we were on the other side, I could hear them again.

"You can help find the parts we require or die trying." She giggled and smiled, not a hint of cynicism or maliciousness in her voice. I was beginning to see why this whole happy joy thing got under Lin's skin. Even I was getting creeped out. "Find a way to assist your people and perhaps you will have a place among your family again as well."

She laid a hand on his arm in a gesture of kindness and encouragement, but Lin jerked away and stalked into the airlock, glaring at her with enough malice to murder small puppies.

"I am sure he will calm down once you are underway." Alma turned to us, still smiling as she spread her arms wide and pulled Lois and I in for a hug. Neither of us expected the unorthodox gesture so our arms were trapped at our sides making the whole thing stiff and awkward, but Alma didn't seem to mind. Her wings fluttered open with glee and she held on tight, wiggling with delight.

Definitely creepy.

"Buttercup boosted your batteries as much as she could,

but you may want to, you know ..." I stepped away from Alma and gestured to the party raging behind us. "Slow down with the festivities, at least until we get back. Buttercup said she could only do it once. Something about incompatible couplings and a fried charger interface."

Alma only smiled and shrugged, fluttering her wings at us again. "Life is meant to be experienced, not survived. Safe travels. If this is to be our last meeting, we were well met. I hope to see you when you return."

Alma ushered us into the airlock and closed the door, waving us off with an enthusiastic sweep of her arm. Even though she knew we might not make it back in time to save her or her crew, she never lost her smile. It was all too surreal. Lois and I waved as the airlock re-pressurized, and Buttercup opened her side of the dock. We walked through, and the Peeri were gone, left to frolic and party as if it were truly the end of days.

I pulled the scarf off Bubbles' head and looked down at her.

"I am very cross with you, young lady," I said as the three of us turned to make our way toward the bridge. "We are going to have to set some ground rules if you are going to live under my roof. No snacking in bed, absolutely no boys, ever, and no folding into space without permission."

Lin scoffed. "You are speaking to that thing as if it were a child."

"We speak to you as if you were a child." Lois reached out and took the scarf from my hand and shoved it back into her purse. "But we like her."

Lois kept walking and I looked over at Lin. "You might want to try being nicer to everyone here. This whole, we're humans and Buttercup is bio-intelligence, is getting old. We're all different. Even you. Get over it."

I followed Lois up to the bridge not caring whether Lin came or not. Let him sulk. Better that than having him insulting everyone.

I wasn't even to my chair before I heard a voice behind me. Lin cleared his throat and stepped forward holding himself erect in the Peeri posture I had come to recognize.

"Pardon me," Lin said. "If I may speak. I believe I owe you all an apology. My actions have been unconscionable, and I am sorry. You saved my life and are now working to save the lives of my people and for that I thank you. I know you do not understand what it is to be Peeri, but please know my only desire is to protect my civilization. I have failed thus far, but if you allow me, I will seek to assist you in any way I can. I still believe the artifact is a detrimental discovery, however it is not for me to decide alone. We will endeavor to bring it back to Lillora where it can be studied, and its fate will be decided there."

Lin stood just inside the bulkhead, wings slicked against his back, staring straight ahead as if he were standing at attention.

I looked at Lois and she smiled at me.

"Welcome to the crew," I said. "Have a seat. You are going to make everyone nervous if you keep standing there like that."

I motioned to the chair Bubbles had occupied earlier and Lin strode over to sit without a word. Friendly might be a stretch, but at least we weren't enemies anymore.

I set Bubbles down in my chair and then looked up to see Twitch camouflaged in a perfect interpretation of the leather on the back. He sat unmoving and would have been all but invisible, had I not become accustomed to spotting him.

"And where have you been?" I chided. "You were supposed to be watching Bubbles. What happened?"

Twitch scurried around and clung to the side of the chair

and reconfigured his camouflage, apparently unwilling to reveal himself.

I reached out to scratch him on the head. "It's okay. Maybe you can keep her more distracted next time."

Twitch turned to his usual red and blue and scurried up to the top of the chair again, chittering a stream of irritated noises as if to say he was doing just that when she folded anyway.

I laughed. "Okay, it's not your fault. Thanks for trying."

Twitch huffed and leapt off the chair. I don't know if there was a way to sulk-glide but he managed it beautifully as he landed on my shoulder, then curled up in an angry ball to glare out at the world.

"So, are you going to let us in on your plan?" Lois asked. "You told Alma we would bring her the parts she needed, but how are we going to get them? I don't think Amazon delivers out here and even if they did, we don't have any money ... space money. What did you call them? Galaxy Credits?"

"Close," Buttercup said. "They are Galactic Credits, and you are correct in assuming we have next to none. Unfortunately, our accounts were exhausted in our efforts to stop the Scavid from obtaining the Viraquin."

"Okay, so how are we going to get the parts we need?"

"Buttercup, how good is that cloak of yours?" I smiled. "I mean, you're a pirate ship, right? We're going to do what pirates do best. We're going to pillage and plunder."

The viewscreen on the front of the bridge turned white and started flashing in a starry spectacle.

"Yes," Buttercup ground out the single word in a shout of excitement. "This is a good plan."

"Alright." I laughed as Lois and I both shaded our eyes with our hands. "Easy with the pyrotechnics."

"Apologies. I am eager to get started."

"Yeah," I chuckled. "I got that."

"I don't want to rob people." Lois looked far less enthused about the idea.

"We're not robbing, we're reappropriating, and it's for a just cause. Plus, I think I may have the perfect target. The good thing is, we won't have to risk exposing Bubbles to any more aliens.

"Buttercup." I turned my attention back to the screen. It had switched to a view of space, but there were rows of sparkling lights chasing all around the frame like a Las Vegas billboard. It seemed she could not contain her excitement completely.

"Are there any repair depots within a reasonable distance of where we found Lin. One that could handle a major rebuild? The seedier the better."

"Yes, there are three."

"Excellent," I said. "Plot a course and get ready. It's time for us to go hunting."

SEVENTEEN

"I believe this is a bad idea." Lin walked along behind us pushing a mop/sponge in a rolling bucket.

"You're only saying that because it hasn't worked yet." I smirked and headed to the dock where several ships were moored.

Just as Buttercup had said, there were three space stations in easy flight range from where we picked up Lin's pod. We visited the other two first. They were well lit and friendly looking with professional staff and fancy neon lighting. I knew without even stopping that our mark would be at neither.

Space Station Tennen was the kind of backwater truck stop everyone except mass chainsaw murderers passed by. If there were a *Friday the 213th*, it would be filmed here. Shadows upon shadows fell in every corner, rust and slime pervaded each surface and patrons and staff all seemed content to glare rather than speak to one another. It was one of the most inhospitable places I had ever seen in my life, and the perfect place for a guy like Olamer to get his ship repaired.

"These coveralls smell like ..." Lois sniffed the collar of her dingy yellow uniform. "I don't even know. Fish, maybe?"

"That smell is not fish," Lin said. "I am just happy we didn't find enough coveralls for all of us."

I sniffed my own collar and winced. "Wait, if that's not fish, what is it?"

"Unauthorized, unauthorized."

A digitized voice came from our left and I looked over to see a strange looking robot speeding our way on a single large wheel. Its body was a rusty metal cabinet, while the head was a dirty ceramic disk that lit up red every time it said the word, unauthorized.

The bot skidded in front of us, like a clown riding a unicycle, never quite stopping. He just fidgeted back and forth, over and over again to keep his balance.

"Unauthorized. Exit area. Unauthorized."

"This is a series two security monitor." Buttercup droned into my ear. "They are annoying but effective watchdogs for the real security in the area. Do not make it angry."

"What do I do?"

"This was your plan," Buttercup said. "I wanted to destroy the station and pull the parts out like a buffet, but you said no, you wanted to do it the hard way. Pirates use guns you know. Guns and swords. Not mop buckets."

"I don't think Buttercup is onboard with our plan," I whispered out of the side of my mouth to Lois.

"Just so you know, the jury is still out over here too."

I looked over my shoulder at Lin.

"Me three."

"Wow. Ye have little faith." I cleared my throat and adjusted my new backpack. It was a hard-shell carrier that Buttercup designed and built using her onboard construction algorithm. She had the ability to build any number of amazing things, provided she had the time, knowhow, and base elements to do it. It was by no means a fast process and it required more power than the eastern seaboard, but it was a handy skill to have when you were out in space with no Walmart in sight.

Inside the pack I carried our precious cargo. The walls were perforated and somehow, Buttercup made it so Bubbles could see out while no one could see in. It was like the best two-way glass I'd ever seen, only it wasn't glass, it was metal, and Buttercup said it was strong enough to withstand an intermediate impact. I didn't have time to ask her to define intermediate. I just hoped we didn't need to find out.

The hope was if we were all together, Bubbles would not be tempted to fold again to find us. As long as the top remained secure, the sleek aerodynamic looking pack seemed as unassuming as any other form of casual space luggage. And it even matched my yellow jumpsuit.

"We are the contract janitorial crew for ..." It occurred to me I didn't know the name of Olamer's ship.

I reached into my bucket full of miscellaneous cleaning materials and a well camouflaged Twitch handed me out an old school clipboard. Somehow that little guy always knew just what I needed. Apparently, no one anywhere in the universe got away from filling out documents in triplicate. I flipped through a few random papers to stall while I muttered to myself.

"Let's see, I have the name for the ship here somewhere ..."

Nothing but silence from Buttercup. I tried again.

"Sorry about this. If you can just give me a moment, the name of the ship should be right here ..."

Still nothing.

I cleared my throat way too loud and then all but shouted.

"If only I could find the name of the ship on this paperwork, I could tell this nice series two security monitor where we are headed!"

"Oh," Buttercup finally said. "Are you referring to me? Why didn't you say so? Olamer's ship is the Crooked Foot.

"Say again?"

"His ship is called the Crooked Foot. In his culture it means something like a bad omen."

I shrugged. "Oh, here it is. The ship is the Crooked Foot. Belongs to an Olamer. I guess he had an altercation on the bridge. The kind that doesn't come off the walls too well if you know what I mean."

I went to give the bot a good-hearted nudge with my fist, but it backed away, avoiding contact. "Do not touch."

I held my hands up in apology. "Sorry, just being friendly. So, are we authorized? We will be in and out in a jiff."

"Sanitization operations prohibited during maintenance. Maintenance delay noted. Commence sanitization. Notify when complete."

I gave the bot a thumbs up as he wheeled backward to allow us to pass. "Will do little buddy. Thanks."

The three of us hurried forward amongst a rush of speeding bots, sparking welders and hydraulic lifts. The ships in dock were not gigantic, but they were bigger than Buttercup, making them impressive to see. One looked like an old junker with hundreds of random rusty parts all welded together to form a disjointed blocky spacecraft. Another was a sleek, mirrored, teardrop that looked as if it could slip through time itself. Automated repair drones worked at inhuman speeds sealing, attaching, repairing and rewiring. Blasted or broken components were replaced with new ones. Old parts were flashed into some sort of incinerator that vaporized them into their basic elements in a matter of seconds. If I weren't in such a hurry, I could have watched for hours. It was all I could do not to gawk like a country boy on his first trip to the city.

"Olamer's ship should be the last one at the end of the dock," Buttercup said, guiding us forward. "Do not walk in the yellow striped areas. Those are bot-ways. They will run you down if you wander in there."

"Seriously?" Lois jumped off a yellow stripe and hurried to catch up. "That seems a little unsafe."

"Productivity gives way to safety in a place like this." Buttercup sounded as if she admired the idea. "It is survival of the fittest. Keep your wits and you will be fine. Wander around thinking everyone here owes you something, and you might end up dead."

"Harsh." Lois kept looking around, making sure she walked in the right place. So did I.

"Here we are." The gangplank to Olamer's ship was down and open, leading straight into the belly of the beast. "No turning back now. Let's do this and get out before someone sees us."

The three of us hurried forward and entered Olamer's ship. The inside was nothing like Buttercup. While she was all sleek icy blue lines and elegant styling, Olamer's ship was more like the inside of a mechanical room basement with exposed conduit, ducting and wires everywhere. The floors were made of a heavy steel grate, and the walls a grimy corrugate. Handrails kept the occupants away from the exposed workings strung along the walls, and steam flowed from several places on the ceiling, making the yellowed light even less effective in the curved, confined spaces.

"Well at least we won't have to open anything to find the

couplings." I looked up and down the entry, taking in the industrial space. "Any idea where the engine room might be?"

"It is likely to the rear." Lin pointed to our left. "The Crooked Foot has two independent engines that would require a central control unit. We should find what we need there."

I ushered him forward with a flourish of my hand. "Lead the way, good prince."

He sniffed in a way I decided was almost a laugh and led us deeper into the ship. Every few feet was a door, something similar to what you would see on a submarine. I assumed they were designed for the same purpose, to seal off and compartmentalize a section if there were a hull breach. Ducking through each one made the trip difficult, especially for someone of my stature. I could not imagine what it was like for Olamer. A cyclops was tall, or at least they were supposed to be. I had to duck to almost half my height every time I went through one of the doorways. Seemed like a bad design for such a large species.

Lin opened one last door and revealed what we were looking for. Even I recognized the more elaborate workings and heavy casings that indicated an engine or power plant of some kind.

"This way." Lin led us straight to a section of long thick cables and sealed metal cabinets. "The power couplings will be in there."

I nodded and reached into my bucket where we had stashed the tools Lin said we would need. I tried to spot Twitch among the jumble then heard him chitter as one of the wrenches levitated out of the bottom of the bucket. His camouflage all but flawless. "Okay, let's get to work. Lin, you and I are on the power couplings, Lois you keep an eye on the hall and make sure no one is coming."

"Why do I have to be the lookout?"

Lin ignored the comment and went to work opening the first cabinet.

"I don't know. Would you rather do this? I can be the lookout if you are fast with a wrench."

"No." Lois crossed her arms. "I hate tools. I just didn't want to be the lookout because I am a woman."

"Excuse me." We all spun toward the bulkhead door to see a large stranger wearing an angry red jumpsuit. He had the words Mechanic Supervisor printed across the left breast, and the expression on his face was anything but friendly.

"You're not supposed to be in here."

EIGHTEEN

W e stood staring at each other for several seconds. The mechanic supervisor was anything but human, and I didn't recognize his species from anything I knew in Earth folklore either. He had four arms, gray skin and a thick black mohawk that grew naturally rather than being shaved or styled that way. Brilliant orange tattoos adorned his heavily muscled arms, and he smoked a bright, green leaf cigar. I could smell it now that he was in the room and the smoke gave off a spicy aroma that reminded me of old leather and cinnamon.

"Speak up," He bellowed. "How did you get past the security droids? You have three seconds to answer before I call security. Maintenance is scheduled for another hour and sanitization is prohibited during maintenance."

All my thoughts went to Bubbles riding shotgun in the pack behind me. This Gray had us trapped. Panic seized my chest and words caught in my throat. If we were all captured, no one would be free to keep her safe. She would be in the hands of some of the worst dregs in the galaxy and it was all our fault. I couldn't believe we had made such an irresponsible miscalculation.

I gauged my chances on running or rushing the huge Gray, but neither option was good. He had blocked our only exit and I couldn't reach for any kind of a weapon without him seeing. Trying to fight him bare-handed would be like a kitten picking a fight with a gorilla, but I was about to try it anyway when Lin turned on his heel and waved his arms in a casual distraction. The motion allowed him to palm the wrench so Gray couldn't see it. His sleight of hand was impressive. If I hadn't known better, I would have thought the tool had never been there at all. If things didn't work out here, Lin could have a promising career as an amateur magician. "We were cleared by a security monitor. It said maintenance had been delayed and we had a sanitization window to work with. We wanted to make up time while we had the chance. We are behind schedule on the Alerian cruiser out there and wanted to get ahead on this detail to make up for it."

Gray nodded his head in understanding. "Those security drones are always screwing up the docket. We did have a materials setback, but we managed to find the parts we needed, and I set the maintenance drones back on cycle to finish the job. The schedule probably didn't update with the new information."

Lin smiled and nodded. "Happens to us all the time. We are just about five minutes from finishing in here, then we will vacate the area until your drones are done with their repair cycle. Thank you so much for letting us know."

"Of course. That's my job." Gray smiled.

Lin turned away but Gray stepped forward, closing the distance between all of us to a few feet.

"I do have one other quick question."

Lin turned around to face him and was surprised to see Gray had followed him into the room.

"Why are three sanitization technicians wrenching on the power coupling boxes in the engine control room? Seems to me that might be a little out of your scope. And where is your uniform, Stretch? Last I heard, The Peeri didn't really do menial labor jobs. Why don't you three show me your I.D.s?"

Gray used his four hands to simultaneously pull a large wrench out of his back pocket, slap it into his palm while reaching for a radio that was clipped on the belt at his hip. He held his fourth hand out, ready to receive our identification.

Showoff.

"No problem," I said. "We don't want any trouble."

I reached down to my bucket and plucked it off the ground, rummaging around inside while Lois and Lin patted their pockets.

"The owner mentioned seeing some space slugs crawling around the duct work in there so ..."

That's as far as I got before I pulled out my revolver and shot him.

"Oh my God." Lois skittered back several steps. "Did you just kill him?"

"Finally!" Buttercup laughed. "I thought you would never stop talking. Why didn't you shoot him in the first place?"

Lin just stared down at Gray, seeming to appraise the situation.

"Everyone, calm down. I didn't kill him." I looked into the bucket and winked as I handed my revolver back to Twitch who had provided the weapon at just the right time. He lost his camouflage long enough to give me a tiny thumbs up, then disappeared among the clutter again.

"He's only stunned. But we need to hurry before someone else comes in and sees him lying on the floor."

Lin turned and produced his wrench as if out of thin air, but Lois could not seem to stop looking at the unconscious supervisor.

"Did you really have to shoot him? I mean maybe we could have—"

"Could have what?" I cut her off. "He would have called security or bashed us with that wrench. I chose door number three. This way he'll wake up in a little while, none the worse for wear, and we will have our parts."

Lois scowled. "I guess so."

"I for one think it was a brilliant shot," Buttercup said. "Be glad the revolver was not set to explosive rounds. Sanitization would have been scraping him off the ceiling for hours."

"Disgusting." Lois walked to the door and peeked into the hall. "Let's just get this over with so we can leave."

"Agreed." I looked at Lin in time to see him heft two thick cylindrical looking pieces into the air.

"Done. We can exit the ship."

Lin dropped the cylinders into the bottom of my bucket with a solid thunk missing Twitch as the agile Chitterwall leapt onto my arm then hid back inside. I tested the weight. The pair had to be twenty or more pounds. I hoped the handle would hold up under the strain. If not, we would have to carry them out in the open and that would be a lot harder to explain to security when we had to make our way off the dock.

"This way." Lin led us up the walkway, ducking through one compartment door after the other, steel grates clacking under our feet. We were about halfway to the main gangplank when the interior lights flickered and then the tell-tale sound of speakers crackling echoed throughout the ship.

"Well, hello there my little bobbins. What treachery are you here to weave?"

I recognized the voice immediately. Low and gruff. Full of malice. It was Olamer. He was on the ship, and he knew we were here.

"Imagine my surprise when the security drones notified me that sanitization had boarded my ship. I figured I should rush right over and thank the crew for doing such a bang-up job ... even though I never scheduled them. And what do I find? A gaggle of rodents rummaging around in my nest."

I nodded toward the exit. We all took off running, but the bulkhead door slammed shut in front of us before we could get more than a few steps.

"Now I'm going to show you what happens to anyone who tries to steal from Olamer Rasalas on his own ship!"

NINETEEN

Suddenly, everything got real. This was not a game. Olamer was a dangerous galactic slave trader. He bought and sold lives the way I purchased groceries; and he threw them away just as easily. Now we were all trapped on this ship with him. Not only Lois and Lin, but Twitch and worst of all Bubbles. If he found this innocent life hidden away in the pack on my back, he would stop at nothing to possess her, then sell Bubbles to the highest bidder. I could not let that happen.

"Listen Olamer, let's talk about this." I tried to sound casual, but my breath was heavy with panic and my eyes darted in every direction looking for another escape. I gripped the thin handle to my bucket in a sweaty fist praying my grip would hold against the hefty load. "There's no harm done. You can have your parts back and we'll owe you one. That's not a bad deal, right?"

Laughter bellowed across the speakers at a volume far louder than before, making me shuffle with apprehension. The sound echoed off the walls and ceilings, permeating my skull. It was like being trapped in a funhouse, only there was no fun, and the owner of the house was a psycho murderer bent on our destruction.

"No harm done? I have a reputation to uphold. I could never show my face on Tennen Station if word got out that I allowed a bunch of sewage slugs to set foot on my ship. Every thief, dealer and hitman would try to get one over on Olamer Rasalas. No. The three of you will adorn the bow of my ship as a warning to future raiders. But not before we have a little fun first. What ... say ... you ..."

He shouted the last three words, drawing them out in a terrifying echo, then steam began to flood the section where we stood. We were forced to clamber back the way we came, with Lin in the lead, followed by Lois, then me. The three of us sprinted along the catwalks looking for a new way to turn, but each time we found a way out, the bulkhead door slammed closed, cutting off our escape.

"Buttercup, we're in a bit of trouble here. Can you target the bridge of his ship or something?"

"Not without triggering the on-station defense systems. If I fire on that ship, I would be annihilated before I could say I told you so. Plus, I have no idea if Olamer is even on the bridge. He could be anywhere on the ship, or even controlling this remotely."

The thought that Olamer was not even here was both chilling and hopeful at the same time. He wouldn't have the satisfaction of killing us himself, but he could obliterate his entire ship with us in it and never be in harm's way.

Lin ran past an open doorway and tried to juke his way back at the last second, but it was too late. The door slammed shut, trapping us all in Olamer's rat's maze.

"This is not getting us anywhere!" Lois shouted in panic. "We're just running in circles. Where's he leading us?"

Superheated steam hissed from the rear of the passage, forcing our path forward.

"If you have a better idea, I'm happy to hear it."

We took off running again, but this time Lois held us back from a full sprint. She didn't get much argument from me. The air in the ship's passageways singed my lungs with every breath and the bucket felt like it was full of lead. If I had to go much longer, Olamer wouldn't have to kill me, I'd have a heart attack all on my own. That's when I realized Olamer's plan.

"We have to figure something out," I panted. "Olamer is going to run us till we drop, then boil us alive." Saying it out loud didn't make it any less terrifying, but I was so tired, fear began to take a back seat to exhaustion. If I breathed any harder, my chest would explode.

"I think we can get through that next door." Lois did her best to lower her voice, but she panted as hard as me. Her blonde hair was wet and matted from the steam and it stuck to the sides of her face. "But we are going to need your help Twitch."

Lois told us her plan and I shrugged. It was worth a shot. If this worked, I would buy Twitch as much pizza as he could eat ... next time we were at a place that made pizza.

We got ready to run, but I stumbled, spilling the contents of my bucket onto the grates.

"Come on." Lois sounded more than a little irritated, but I couldn't just leave everything there. I had lugged the uncooperative thing with me this whole time. It contained our precious couplings, not to mention my revolver. If Olamer showed up in person, that could come in super handy.

I scooped up all the important things, then I stood to start running again.

"Hurry up." Lois waved me forward. She and Lin were a

little ahead of me, but they were forced to wait while I lumbered along. I coughed and wheezed, trying to suck in enough air to go on. More steam shot out behind us, raising the temperature and we stumbled forward. There was an open door to our right and Lin made a dive for it, but as usual the door slammed shut before he got there.

More laughter over the speakers as the steam billowed out, making it all but impossible to breathe. Then the door bounced back open. I looked down to see Twitch crouched at the base, holding one of the wrenches from my tool bucket in the jam. The door bounced two more times, then Olamer's laughter cut off.

"Wha ... What did you do? No."

Lois and I pried our hands into the crack and pulled it open again. I pressed my shoulder to the opening while Lois and Lin squeezed though, then Twitch hopped over, and I rolled in. As soon as I was away, and the wrench was free, the door slammed shut, sealing us into the room.

"Gaaaa!" Olamer shouted over the speakers. "That won't save you. I have control of this entire ship. All you have done is lengthened the span of your execution."

"We're in no hurry," I panted. "Take your time. In fact, if you want to get back to us next week ..."

We all stood and Twitch ran up my leg to my shoulder. I held my hand out to him in gratitude.

"High five little man. That was incredible." Twitch slapped my palm with his tiny hand and chittered. "Lois that was fast thinking from you too. I can't believe it worked, but we're not out yet.'

"It appears we have trapped ourselves in the mess hall." Lin wandered around the room looking for an alternate exit, but found none. I saw a door on the opposite side of the room, but

Olamer, no doubt, had control over that one too. We went from being steam broiled to waiting for the cook to come by and do us in with his butcher knife. Either way, we weren't going anywhere.

"Could we crawl through a roof access or a maintenance tunnel?" I put my hands on my knees, trying to catch my breath. "Anything that will get us out of here."

Lin shook his head. "It seems we have chosen the only room to which there is no alternate access. This may double as a security holding area. Many ships utilize spaces in multiple ways."

"Great history lesson, but not much help."

"Do you smell that?" Lois sniffed the air. "It's sort of like ..."

"Gas." I stood up straight and looked for the source. The odor was not quite the same as propane or natural gas, but I was sure that whatever Olamer pumped into the room was every bit as explosive or toxic. I had no idea how it would affect us, much less Twitch and Bubbles.

Lois ran to the door on the far side of the mess hall and clawed at the corner, trying to pry open a finger hold. "We have to get out of here!" Her voice was high and frantic, and I could hear her nails scraping on the metal.

"The cooking fires are almost ready," Olamer taunted. "Do you smell the end coming? You thought you had escaped, but your flesh will burn no matter where you try to hide."

Lin coughed and I began to choke as well. Lois kept scratching at the door, but only lasted a couple of seconds longer before she collapsed to the floor. Lin and I went down too. I couldn't see Bubbles, but Twitch went limp on my shoulder. I had to assume Bubbles wasn't faring any better. The gassy haze hung in the air now. If Olamer didn't destroy his own ship altogether, he would do some massive damage with this explosion. I had doomed us all and there was no way out.

I looked into my bucket, blinking my eyes to try and clear my vision. Was there something in there that could pry the door? I could blast it with my revolver, but that would only speed our demise in the explosive environment.

"Move to the door with Lois." It was Buttercup. I felt so tired and disoriented I forgot all about her.

"What?" I struggled to think. I had my arm up, trying to breathe through the crook of my elbow, but the gas was so thick. I choked and gasped. My head pounded. "What are you talking about?"

"I don't have time to explain. Do what I say. Move to the door with Lois and get ready to run."

I forced myself to my feet and grabbed Lin and the bucket of parts. We staggered to the door where Lois crouched on the ground with her face pressed to the crack of the door, desperate to suck in some fresh air.

"The time is nigh," Olamer said. "Shriek your way to oblivion."

There was a flash of light from the corner and I closed my eyes. Nothing happened. Another flash; sparks from a wiring assembly on the other side of the room. I didn't know how Olamar managed it, or from where, but it didn't really matter.

"What's wrong?" Olamer shouted. "Why isn't this working?"

All at once, the door opened and the three of us tumbled into the open hallway. We were through in an instant, then the door closed behind us.

"Run forward to the second bulkhead door, then go through." Buttercup again.

We gulped in lungs full of stale air. Twitch stirred on my shoulder and I prayed that meant Bubbles was okay too.

I stood, gripping the heavy bucket full of parts in my hand and helped Lin up. Lois heard Buttercup's instructions, so she was already moving.

"Stop!" Olamer shouted. "You can't do this. How are you doing this?"

The speakers crackled into silence and we sprinted forward, taking the second door as instructed. The opening led to what looked like a supply dock.

"You will have to work the airlock from your side. I have docked to Olamer's ship, but you only have a few seconds before he will figure it out and override the connection."

We hurried over, tripping on loose crates and discarded boxes. I struggled to hold onto my bucket. It dragged on me like an anchor, but I wasn't about to lose it now. The room was in complete disarray, but we stumbled to the airlock and opened the hatch. As soon as it closed and pressurized, we were able to open the door to a glorious looking sea of glassy blue. We made our way through as fast as we could, then sealed the door behind us. Now all we had to do was get away before Olamer blasted us to bits.

TWENTY

"**B**uttercup, can't you go any faster?" Lin, Lois and I stood frozen in front of the main display on the bridge. I had Bubbles in my arm and Twitch on my shoulder. The first thing I did once we got underway was check my pack. I had no idea how the rough ride, steam-seared air and toxic gas had affected Bubbles. Part of me wished she would have folded away just to be clear of the mess we were in, but she rode it all out. When I opened the pack, she sat inside looking none the worse for wear, giggly and happy and doing her little light show, as always. I began to wonder if this little Viraquin was a lot tougher than I gave her credit.

"I cannot exit the station on anything other than reserve power. Anything more will trigger the defense systems. At best we will be banned from ever visiting again, at worst we will be shot right out of the sky."

"How long will it take Olamer to get his ship up and running to follow us?" Lois was chewing on her nails. Something I'd never seen her do before. "Can he take a shot at us from the docks somehow?"

"This is Tennen. With the right bribes, to the right people, anything is possible, but if he were going to fire on us, he would have done so already."

"What about following us?" I asked. "He could just shoot us down once we're off the station."

"We removed his power couplings." Of the three of us, Lin was the only one who did not look frantic. He was in as dire straits as the rest of us when we left, but now that we were out, he seemed to be back to his calm, cool, composed self. "He has no active propulsion system until they are replaced. It is a simple repair, but unless he has a spare on hand, it will take time to procure. At least enough time for us to clear the station and warp away."

Lois visibly relaxed and even I felt a little relieved at the realization. Knowing Olamer had no way of riding on our coat tails was comforting to say the least.

"Did we just get away with our first pirate caper?" I grinned.

"Did you just use the word caper?" Lois countered.

"Don't rain on my parade. We did it. We got in and thieved our way into piracy." I could not help but be excited. I would never be happy about taking advantage of the innocent, but someone like Olamer? I would go back and rob his coffers every day.

"Don't get too excited," Buttercup said. "You had a horrible plan, and everyone was at risk. If you're going to survive in this game, you'll have to get much smarter. Most pirates are only famous because they're dead."

"All right, all right, but let's take a moment to celebrate." I clapped Lois on the arm and smiled even broader, eliciting a smile from her as well. "That's better," I said. "We won. Enjoy it. We may not always be so lucky."

"Speaking of luck." Lois set her purse down on her chair, pulled out a brush and began working it through her tangled hair. "I don't understand how we aren't a bunch of deep-fried turkeys. That room was full of gas. Why didn't it spark off like a blast forge?"

"When I docked with the ship, I was able to accomplish passive use of the ship's sensors. Olamer opened a valve to flood the room, but did not take into account the proper air to gas mixture. The atmosphere was so rich with gas it would not light. I had to wait for the concentration to rise even higher because I knew that when I opened the door, I would introduce more oxygen. If I left the door open too long, or if I did not allow the concentration of gas to rise high enough, the room would explode."

I blinked. "So we were that close to being burned alive?"

"Like I said," Buttercup scolded. "You better get smarter or you're going to get dead."

"Well, I'm glad you were able to dock with the ship and take control." Lois nodded. "If it weren't for you, we would have never made it."

"Just remember that next time I want to use the guns from a nice safe distance."

I let out a humorless laugh. "Blasting innocents is not okay."

"That was Tennen," Buttercup countered. "No one on that space station was innocent."

"You did all of that just to find this creature's mother?" Lin peered down at Bubbles in my arms. "It seems like a long way to go for a creature who can hardly communicate with you."

I looked at Bubbles as well, and she met my eyes with a smile, flashing her bioluminescent light faster as she listened to our voices.

"Oh, I think she can communicate just fine. Besides, creatures like this are the ones who need the most help. She's a baby. She can't do anything to defend herself. She's the only true innocent in this room."

"On that point you and I can agree." The new voice came from behind us, and we all spun around to face it. Olamer stood sopping wet and holding a weapon that resembled a sawed-off, four-barreled shotgun.

"Now, no one get twitchy, especially you, Buttercup. You just keep that little arm tucked away in the ceiling and we can all walk away from this thing breathing and in one ... mostly whole piece."

TWENTY-ONE

There were so many things about Olamer that didn't match my preconceived notions that my brain nearly shorted out from the confusion. How could he be here? Why was he three feet tall? And what was that smell?

Everyone, even Lin, smashed a hand over their nose in a desperate attempt to escape the pervasive odor. Twitch was the only one who didn't seem to mind. He just ran around behind my neck and hissed at the unwelcome intruder.

"I hope my pungent bouquet hasn't offended anyone. I am always surprised at the lack of automated security in a ship's septic system. I find if you are willing to go that extra step, you can find your way into just about anywhere."

"Fascinating." I continued to grip my nose as if it might try to escape my face. Right now, I wished it would. "That answers one question. What about your ..."

I would have used a hand to indicate his considerable lack of stature, but one held Bubbles and the other was busy fending off the attack on my olfactory system. I nodded and looked him up and down instead. He seemed to get the picture because his single bulbous eye narrowed and he nudged the gun in my direction.

"You have something to say?"

I leaned back, shaking my head. "No. It's just that on Earth, images of someone such as yourself are a bit more ... statuesque."

"Human folklore is far from accurate," Buttercup chimed in. "For instance, on your world a cyclops is a mighty and terrifying monster, but in reality Olamer is more of a stunted one-eyed version of what your fantasy novels refer to as a dwarf."

"Could we not piss off the smelly guy who just crawled through your septic system with a giant gun?" Lois added a second hand to her face, stunting her nasally voice even further. "He's here. Who cares about his lineage?"

"I am mutually offended and grateful, human female." Olamer tilted a nod in her direction then turned his eyes to me. "You are the captain on this ship, so I am holding you responsible for the assault carried out on me and my vessel."

Lois began to step forward, but I shook my head.

"You attacked without provocation, damaged and stole my property, and now I think we can add personal insults to the list of offenses."

"What do you want Olamer?" Buttercup did not seem cowed by Olamer or his blunderbuss weapon. If anything, she sounded annoyed and petulant despite the fact that he could kill any one of us with the twitch of his finger.

"Revenge?" she continued. "There is no money in it. Your bounty on our Peeri is spoiled too. We've already been to his people, and it turns out, they don't want him any more than we do."

Lin turned to peer at the viewscreen over his shoulder. "Pardon me?"

"You know what I mean," Buttercup snapped. "There is nothing here for you. If you want your parts, take them, but you and I both know it is better to be owed a favor than leave with empty hands."

Olamer laughed, keeping his eyes on me the whole time. "Your ship knows me a little too well I'm afraid. We have had more than a few adventures together haven't we, *Buttercup.*"

He enunciated her name making me wonder just how well ... and how long these two had really known each other.

"Your parts are over there." I tore my hand away from my face just long enough to motion toward the bucket sitting on the floor. "I'm not sure how much good they're going to do. You stowed away on a self-aware ship in the middle of space. It's not like you can open the door and stroll off into the sunset. What are you going to do, float back to Tennen?"

"You let me worry about that. Right now, we are negotiating price. You acquired the goods you needed. Now we need to settle on an item in trade."

"We don't have any money," Lois said. "Not unless ..."

She turned her gaze to Lin.

The Peeri prince eyed her, then turned his attention forward again, holding his nose with his elbow straight out the side, looking almost like a strange salute. The position was so preposterously proper it would have made me laugh were it not for our current situation.

"I am afraid I come with no financial backing. As Buttercup so eloquently put it, I am spoiled merchandise. I can no more elicit funds willingly than I could through ransom."

I threw my arm out to the side as if to illustrate the impasse. "We have nothing of value, and you're stranded. Why don't you put your emotional support gun down and we can talk this out like ... well ... mutual living creatures?"

It wasn't the greatest diplomatic pitch anyone had ever made, but it was the best I had for a one-eyed sewer-stinking slave trader.

Olamer tilted his head to the side and grinned with yellow rotting teeth. "Oh, I believe you can do better than that."

His eyed went to the sleepy bundle resting in my arm. Bubbles had been remarkably quiet during this exchange. Maybe it was because she didn't have the capacity to recognize danger, or maybe it was because she didn't have a nose. Either way, Olamer had his eye on her and that was something I could not ... would not stand for.

I turned my body slightly to shield her from Olamer's view. "No deal. You can have something else. Anything else."

Olamer laughed. "Oh, you should have thought of that before you opened a channel and exposed that beauty to Uncle Olamer. I always keep a recorded log of my transmissions and when I got a glimpse of your baby Viraquin there, I figured it was something special. It took some effort to figure out what it was, but as luck would have it, there is a particular race of artificially intelligent aliens out there who are scouring the universe looking for just this sort of thing. They will pay a pretty penny for yours. More than fair compensation for the parts you require. And like you said, it's always better to part with a little skin on the table. I could even be convinced to owe you a credit or two when this thing is said and done."

"You're disgusting," Lois said. "I can't believe anyone would sell another living breathing creature for profit."

"I believe your people trade in livestock and pets all the time," Lin said, raising an eyebrow.

Lois turned her glare toward him. "That's not the same thing, and you know it."

"Perhaps you should ask their opinion on the subject."

"Enough!" Olamer snapped. "I am taking the infant."

He leveled his weapon at me, then seemed to think better of it and turned the barrel toward Lois. Bring it here or you can watch your crew die one at a time."

"Please don't do this." I did my best to sound assertive, but panic and desperation had seeped into my voice. My knees were weak and all I wanted to do was put myself between Olamer and Bubbles.

"It is already done. Bring ... it ... here." He enunciated each word as if that would make me rise to action.

"Ben, no," cried Lois. She looked at Olamer. "There has to be something else, we'll give you whatever you want."

"I'm not going to ask again." Olamer's voice got louder. "Hand over the infant, or your human female dies."

My legs froze and I gripped Bubbles tighter.

Tension quieted the room to a dead silence, then Olamer's gun exploded with sound. The shot brought with it screams of panic and disbelief from everyone in the room, including me.

"No!" I looked toward Lois, but she was still standing. The panel to her right, ruined from the blast of Olamer's devastating weapon, smoked from the damage.

Lois stared at the panel for a moment then put her face in her hands and sobbed.

"Lois, are you o—"

"Give me the infant!" Olamer shouted.

I turned a hateful gaze toward Olamer. I wanted nothing more than to blast this pint sized mini-monster into bits, but he had us dead to rights. I gathered all my will and managed a small shuffle forward, but that was as far as I got before stopping again to shield Bubbles with my other hand.

"Oh, for the love of ..."

Olamer stepped forward and tried to snatch Bubbles out of

my hands. I shrank from him at first, but he hedged his gun toward Lois again. I had no choice. At least this way no one would die. I just had to hope Bubbles would fold back to us the moment she was out of our sight.

I extended an arm, so shaky I thought I might drop the innocent little infant to the ground. I used my other hand to steady her, and Bubbles looked at me with sad unsure eyes. Then Olamer reached out to grab her, jerking his prize out of my protective arms like a cub from its den.

Bubbles twisted and squirmed until she was able to look at me again. Her eyes were full of shock and betrayal. My heart stopped and pain beat inside of my chest instead.

"It'll be okay. Don't worry. I'll come get you."

Olamer chuckled and a crackle of noise sent electricity through Bubbles' tiny body. The bioluminescent light on her skin went white for a second, then her eyes closed, and for the first time since I had seen her, she went dark all over.

"You bastard!" I screamed and stepped forward. "What did you do?"

I was surprised to find Lin at my side, holding me back by my shoulder. "Stun gloves."

I looked at Olamer's hands. He wore something akin to yellow leather work gloves, but it seemed they hid a more sinister purpose.

"She will be fine." Lin squeezed my shoulder a little tighter to remind me not to do something reckless. "They stun the victim for a limited duration of time."

"That's right." Olamer had his eyes on us, but his gun was still on Lois. She had moved her hands to her mouth to control her sobs, her tear-filled eyes locked on Bubbles' limp body.

"Listen to the good Peeri prince. He may just keep you all alive a little longer."

"I am picking up an approaching ship," Buttercup interrupted. "Arges class. It is the Crooked Foot."

I stared at Olamer in horror and disbelief, drawing his grin into a wide beaming smile.

"My ship is equipped with a tracker program. If I ever find myself separated from it, she will come running to the rescue. Not quite as intelligent as Buttercup, but I don't have to put up with all the lip either. The repairs were all but completed on Tennen. I have a standing account at the docks, so I knew they would replace the power couplings you stole from me. I'm sure they won't be happy about her unscheduled departure, but once I sell this little beauty." He wiggled Bubbles in his hand. "I will have plenty of credits to buy my way back into port."

"Let her dock and revert all controls to manual in the cargo bay." Olamer bellowed out the order. He was done with pleasantries. He had what he wanted and was determined to get away.

We all stood for several tense moments, then Buttercup responded with a single bitter reply. "Done."

Olamer took a step back and turned his gun arm over to peer at one of the bracers on his forearm. It came to life in a scrolling script of green text, then he smiled again.

"Good," he said. "I would say it has been a pleasure but ..." He sniffed himself and winced. "I owe you for making me endure this indignity as well."

He turned his gun onto the bridge and pulled the trigger. Bright yellow bolts scattered out from the barrels, spraying the bridge controls and viewscreen with destruction. Lois, Lin and I hit the floor as he pulled the trigger again and again, laughing like a maniacal sailor. Glass, shards of Buttercup's hull and pieces of the viewscreen, crashed to the floor as he rendered the bridge to ruins. The sound, deafening booms in my ears.

When it was over, Olamer turned and ran off the bridge, still laughing as he disappeared down the corridor.

I scrambled to my feet and turned toward the screen. "Buttercup, are you there? Are you alright?"

I ran to the ruined screen and put my hand on the shattered control display that resided in front of my captain's chair.

Lois came up beside me and started pressing her hand to the spiderwebbed surface as well, but I was already turning to run in the other direction. I sprinted through the rear door to the bridge and skidded around the corner to the open access to the cargo hold. I had just enough time to see Olamer's ship undock and float away in a rush of steam and air. I imagined he was still laughing inside that ship. Laughing at the fact that he had gotten away and left us floating in space, doomed to die.

TWENTY-TWO

"Buttercup answer me." I could hear Lois screaming on the bridge, but I could hardly tear my eyes away from the spot where Olamer's ship had disappeared from view. I couldn't believe it. Bubbles was gone, and I had just handed her over, like a sack of old groceries.

"Buttercup please." Lois's voice came to me again, but this time it jolted me out of my fog. Bubbles was not the only one who was in trouble. Buttercup had sustained massive damage. If she was gone too ...

I forced myself to turn away from the viewport and face the reality that I may have lost not one, but two of the most important beings who had ever come into my life.

I ran, but my feet felt like stones. I wanted to curl into a little ball and pretend all of this hadn't happened. That I hadn't caused it to happen. Why did I have to steal those parts, worse, why had I decided on Olamer as our target? Now Bubbles and Buttercup were in terrible danger. I had to play pirate and now others were suffering the consequences.

When I jogged onto the bridge, I saw Lois standing before

the display screen, both hands splayed against the ruined surface. She sobbed in big, angry breaths and her head was turned just enough for me to see the tears streaming down her face. Lin seemed to be systematically touching every screen, button or lever on the bridge. None if it seemed to be working. The screens did not flare to life, the buttons did not light, and levers did not ... do whatever levers were supposed to do.

I hurried forward and put a hand on Lois's shoulder while I used the other to try and pull her hands away from the shattered view screen.

"You're going to cut yourself." I lifted one hand away then the other without much resistance, then I walked her over to her chair.

Twitch glided in out of nowhere and landed on my shoulder and made a sad squeaking little noise as Lois tried to compose herself.

"What are we going to do now?" She caught her breath several times, then she inhaled deeply and managed to get herself under control. "We're out here all alone. We can't help Bubbles, we can't help Lin's people, we can't even save ourselves."

I opened my mouth to say something, but nothing came out. She was right. I should have done more to stop Olamer. Should have done more to stop all of this from happening.

"We aren't going to give up." I turned away from Lois and started pounding on the touchscreen panels myself, picking up where Lin had left off. "This isn't over. We're still alive. There must be something we can do. I'm so sorry I dragged you into all of this, Lois. As soon as I figure something out, I promise I'll—

"You will what?" The tone in Lois' voice had that no nonsense grit she reserved for frightening grizzly bears. She stood and I turned to see her expression had switched from desperation to anger. Something I said flipped a switch and now she wiped away her tears ready for a fight.

"You'll drop me off? Take me home? Let me tell you something, Ben Roberts, I'm here because I chose to be. You aren't my caretaker and you're not getting rid of me so you can ease your conscience. This situation sucks but I'm in it with you, so stop acting like I'm some sort of fragile baggage."

I stood silent for a moment then nodded. "You're right. I'm sorry. I couldn't ask for a better person to be stranded helplessly in space with."

Lois narrowed her eyes at me then let out a snicker as a grin cracked her face. "Is it possible for you to be serious about anything?"

"I'm serious about figuring a way out of this mess."

I turned to look at Lin, who had apparently exhausted his exploratory efforts on the bridge. He stood stiff and proper next to my captain's chair with a genuine look of concern on his face. "Perhaps we can access Buttercup from somewhere else on the ship."

I started to nod, thinking this might be the first good idea anyone had come up with since Olamer went postal on the bridge. I turned, ready to head toward Buttercup's engineering section when Lois pointed at the viewscreen behind me. When I followed her gaze around, I saw a small unruined corner of the main screen come to life. It was only about a thirteen-inch square, but seeing even that much made my heart soar with hope.

"Buttercup?"

Lois and I hurried closer so we could see. Lin lost his stoic expression as well and stepped forward with wide-eyed anticipation. The little square section turned green, then black again then it showed a shrunken image of the space outside the ship.

"Next time I see Olamer I'm going to make him wish he'd never crawled out from under whatever rock he was born under."

Lois leapt into the air and all three of us crowded around the tiny screen, staring at it as if it were a newborn child.

"Buttercup, I thought we had lost you." I spoke first.

"Are you okay?" Lois asked.

"Are all of your systems still operational?" Even Lin couldn't hide his concern, either for the life-support systems on the ship or for Buttercup herself.

"I am still operational. I was forced to shut down all systems here on the bridge, but overall systems are still functioning."

"But Olamer ..." Lois started to recount the horrific events that played out just a few minutes earlier, then couldn't seem to finish.

"Olamer is destructive and ruthless, but he is not very smart. Much of the navigational and crew interface systems are located here on the bridge, but my main processing center is housed in a much more secure section of the ship. Only a simpleton would think destroying the bridge could kill me."

I did not point out the fact that there were three, four including Twitch, very worried simpletons staring at her screen who feared that very thing.

"So, what are we going to do now?" Lois said. "Do we need to get you to a space station somewhere?"

"Perhaps we could return to Tennen." Lin looked away from the screen to Lois. "I realize it was a lawless community, however, they did seem to have competent repair crews."

"There is no time for that," I snapped. "We have to go after Olamer."

Lois and Lin both turned their eyes on me.

"Don't give me that look. He has Bubbles. We're going after him. We have to help her. Buttercup, when can you get underway?"

"Hold on a sec." Lois raised her hands. "Let's calm down a second and think through a plan."

"Think through a plan?" I glared at her. "Bubbles is in trouble. Don't you even ca—"

Lois stepped forward and put her finger in my face. "If you know what's good for you, you will not finish that sentence. Of course I care about Bubbles. I also care about us and about Buttercup and about the Peeri stuck on that ticking time bomb of a ship. Much as we might like to ignore everything else, there are a lot more things to think about that just Bubbles."

I ground my teeth and breathed heavily through my nose. She was right of course, but logic and emotion seldom made good bedfellows. I cared about all those things, but they all seemed like a dim comparison to the urgent worry I felt for Bubbles now that she was in the hands of that one-eyed slave trader. If I had to get out and walk, I would go after her until I was sure she was safe, or I was dead.

"My systems are all operational and I am able to self-repair, however it will take some time."

"How much time?" I asked, ignoring Lois's glare.

"Approximately three hours. The bridge will be nowhere near operational, but I will be able to facilitate navigational drives and the Warpstream Generator. I can continue repairing enroute, though the speed at which I can self-replicate will be diminished due to the power consumption of the Warpstream Generator."

"Good." I nodded, then my eyes went to Lin and shame washed over me. His people were out there too. They were waiting for our help. Without us they would perish. At least anyone who wanted Bubbles would want to keep her alive.

"How long before the Peeri ship runs out of life support power?" I kept my eyes on Lin.

"Forty-seven hours," Buttercup responded without hesitation.

"Excellent." Hope washed over me again. "That gives us a large window of time to work with. Now all we have to do is figure out where Olamer went."

"There is no need," Lin answered. "If Olamer intends to traffic Bubbles for profit, there are only a few places he can do so without raising suspicion, and only one is within a reasonable travel distance to our location."

"I concur with Prince Lintang," Buttercup said. "When his ship docked to my hull, I placed a tracker beacon on his airlock, but it was not necessary. He is headed straight for the Shedu system. The Fafnir Space Station is the largest and most lawless area in the universe. Even the A.S.S. does not patrol there."

"Olamer will make his trade there," Lin finished. "And no one is likely to question him."

"Okay." I nodded. "We can get underway as soon as Buttercup is ready."

"How long will it take to get there?" Lois looked at Buttercup's small screen.

"Olamer's ship is faster than I am. He can produce more power so he will arrive sooner, but I should be able to make the trip in eighteen hours."

I nodded. That was still okay. Still, plenty of time to make our rescue and get back to Lin's ship.

"And how long to make the trip from Fafnir to the Peeri ship?"

"Approximately twenty-six hours at maximum speed."

That wide open window of opportunity slammed town to a crack as I did the math in my head.

"Giving us three hours to find Olamer, rescue Bubbles and get away again."

Lois and I both looked to Lin.

"We must save the child." He made the statement as if there were no other possible answer. "Her capture was a direct result of trying to help my people, or rather me and the mistake I made in trying to forestall their advance to my planet. I still do not agree with their mission, but I have no wish to see them perish under my watch either. Having said that, the captain and crew on that ship are able-bodied explorers who knew the risks of their profession. Bubbles is an innocent. We should save the innocent, and if at all possible, we will return to my ship and assist them afterwards."

Lin was so matter of fact about the statement it was almost chilling, but he was right. Bubbles was an innocent and a nearly helpless one at that. We were all she had, and I for one, was prepared to do just about anything to get her back.

"Agreed then," Lois said. "I think it's the right call, too. I just wanted to make sure we all knew what we were getting into."

She looked to me and raised an eyebrow. "What are your orders Captain?"

I narrowed my eyes at her trying to decide if she was being facetious, then looked to the screen.

"Make your repairs as fast as possible. We have a meeting to crash and Olamer is going to learn screwing with us is far more painful than he thinks."

TWENTY-THREE

"I am more than capable of handling myself in a strange place," I said, as we stepped into Buttercup's airlock. "I have been to a dive bar or two in my time. I am not an idiot."

I straightened my brown synth-leather jacket and admired the heavy cloth pants and boots on my feet. Buttercup radioed Fafnir ahead of our arrival and arranged for some *space appropriate* clothing to be delivered to our slip when we arrived. I had something that looked like a light-weight bomber jacket, canvas-like pants and boots. Lois wore something similar, though her outfit was much more colorful in keeping with her style. She wore a red coat and dark colored pants and canary yellow boots. When I said her outfit might be a little loud for a group trying to keep a low profile, she said I should mind my own business. Buttercup could have a great career in fashion if she ever wanted to give up the pirate game.

Lin's disguise was more subtle. A long plum colored coat with a deep hood that hid his face. I wasn't sure if anyone would recognize him, but something told me Peeri didn't frequent a place like this. Just seeing him might raise a few eyebrows.

Buttercup didn't seem concerned about anyone looking twice at a couple of humans. She said we weren't the first to pop up out here and we would not be the last. Usually, humans were abducted as a curiosity and traded on the slave market, so it wouldn't be out of the realm of possibility for a human to be here. The one thing everyone did seem to worry about was me.

"Do not speak to or interact with anyone," Buttercup said. "This is not a friendly place, especially when it seems friendly."

"Okay." The airlock door closed behind us and Lois eyed me along with Lin. The silence inside the area while it equalized was deafening.

"I said, okay." I raised my hands and shrugged off their accusing stares. "I'll behave. No rash actions. I promise I will run my every word through committee first."

Lois grinned. "It's a start."

She looked forward just as the airlock door opened onto the Fafnir Space station, squashing any thoughts of a reply. This place was nothing at all like Tennen. That old truck stop was more of a dingy rest area for repairs and refueling, this was a bustling metropolis full of ... well, not so much people, but lots of life.

I led everyone up the busy dock toward the main street. There were shops, kiosks, advertisements and holograms everywhere I looked. My senses were assaulted with bright colors, neon lights and a warm stale breeze that carried a million smells I didn't recognize. I just wanted to stop and look around. To take it all in and try to process all the sights and sounds, but there wasn't time. We had to move forward. Finding Olamer, and getting Bubbles back was our priority, and to do that, we had to keep our boots in motion.

"Everyone act natural, and no one will pay us any attention," I said. "There is so much going on here, there's no way anyone will notice us unless we're stupid enough to make a scene."

"Great advice for *all of us* to follow."

I looked back and shot Lois a sardonic smile. She grinned as she forged along ahead of Lin. Her eyes darted in every direction like mine. I was worried her clothes would stand out, but in truth, she blended in better than I did. Everyone wore colors bright enough to shock a clown convention. I would have been better off wearing a yellow headband and a turquoise belt.

Dangerous as it might be, this was an incredible experience. I wanted to know more. What was it like to live in a place like this? How did everyone get along? I mean, how bad could they be. They all had to live together, right?

We continued through the galaxy equivalent of Times Square and I glanced over my shoulder at my crew and smiled. Lois met my eye and started to smile back, but then her eyes went wide, and she pointed ahead of me.

I spun around just in time to run smack into a huge, crimson-skinned alien. I was six-foot four and not of a slight build, but this guy made me feel like a grade-schooler at an NFL draft. He towered over me by at least six inches and his arms were easily the size of my thighs. Deep, blue veins were visible on his neck, up his face and all along his bald head and they seemed to be getting darker and more pronounced. He panted and growled in fury, pumping his fists and staring at me with dark blue eyes.

"Slap him." Buttercup shouted in my mind.

"Come again?" I took a step back, preparing myself to duck and run, hoping this guy was not half as fast as he looked.

"I told you not to interact with anyone," she scolded. "Slap him right across the face. It is their custom. An apology for wrongdoing or insults. Do it or this mission is going to end with him pulling your arms off at the shoulders."

I took a deep breath and steadied myself. "Okay, sorry about this my man." Then I flattened my hand and slapped the huge, red creature across the face. He turned his head for a second, absorbing the gentle pat, then turned his eyes to me looking more murderous than ever.

"Harder and mean it." Buttercup sounded urgent, almost panicked. "You just gave him the equivalent of a sniveling half-hearted apology. Slap him like you mean it, right now, or say goodbye to ever being able to wipe your own ..."

I hauled back and hit the huge alien with a haymaker that would have put me on the ground, open handed or not. My palm stung and my fingers hurt. That was all the apology I had to give. If that wasn't enough, then big red would have to go about getting his satisfaction the hard way.

This time when he turned his head to look at me, he showed a row of black teeth in a smile. He nodded, and for a second, I thought he might return my apology with an acceptance slap that would make me sorry I hadn't gone with plan B. Instead, he shoved me out of the way so he could continue walking without saying another word.

"Watch where you're going." Lois punched me in the arm as if she wanted to get in on some of the action. "Why do you have to be so stubborn all the time?"

I tried to think of something to say, but had nothing, so I rubbed my sore hand, turned and kept walking.

"You are quite fortunate that Bane accepted your apology." Lin sounded more informative than scolding, but my bruised ego couldn't tell the difference. "They are well known for their temper and willingness to act upon it."

I nodded. "Good to know. Do not bump into the Bane at an outlaw spaceport unless you want your arms ripped off at the sockets. I should write some of this stuff down."

We wove our way through the throng of aliens. There were tall ones and short ones. Some hairy and some covered in moss or slime. I was surprised at how many had a bipedal form. They all seemed to resemble humans, however loosely, in that respect. Very few had anything like tentacles or slithered like a snake. They all seemed to have arms and legs and stood upright to use their hands, be it one, two or six.

I was also amazed at how many species I recognized from folklore. I had already seen Lin the fairy and Olamer the cyclops/dwarf. But then there was Bane the demon, something that looked like bigfoot, a woman with snakes for hair, I refused to look at her, and even a dog-headed humanoid that shouted ancient Egyptian mythology.

I couldn't imagine what we would see here in an afternoon of people watching ... er, alien watching.

"Your first destination is ahead on the right," Buttercup informed us. "It is a bar and brothel called the Black Star. The establishment is known as being a hub for lowlifes and derelicts like Olamer. It is likely he will try to initiate a contact to sell Bubbles here."

Hearing her say it like that made my blood boil so hot I wanted to lash back, but it wasn't her fault. Olamer was the one we were after. He was the one who deserved my anger, not Buttercup.

"What should we do once we're inside?" I pointed to the sign when I spotted it ahead. It said Black Star in white neon then flashed a star-shaped black light underneath it.

"I suggest you go straight to the bartender. He will be your best source for information."

"Got it."

I reached out to grab a door handle and open the door, but there was none. I pressed on the dark glass, but the door would not budge.

"I think the place might be closed."

Lin sighed and stepped forward. He laid his hand to a silver plate to the right of the door and the one-way glass slid open to the side, revealing a dark, dreary interior bustling with aliens all staring at me.

"Try to blend in, remember," Lois said, as she followed Lin into the bar.

"Try to blend in," I mocked in a childish voice, and fell in behind her. The door closed and we were inside.

"One more thing, Ben," Buttercup said. "While you're in here, don't piss anyone off."

TWENTY-FOUR

I looked around the bar as everyone inside had a chuckle over my door debacle and then went back to the drinks and chatter. I was surprised at how much the place resembled a dive bar on earth. Granted the walls were adorned with the heads of several animals I didn't recognize, but other than that, it felt oddly familiar to the Buzzard's Roost back home. There were gaming tables in the far corner, mismatched chairs everywhere and high-backed booths along the walls. The ceiling was all exposed HVAC, wires and conduit, painted black and lit with strategically placed backlights. Over the bar hung another of the stylized stars with backlighting as well. The place was dark, smoky, loud and menacing for anyone who didn't belong. Pretty much every dive bar in America as far as I was concerned.

"I don't know why you all think I'm going to be the one to get us in trouble here." I walked past Lin, who was getting ready to sit at a table, and headed straight for the bar. "That thing on the street was an accident. It could have happened to either one of you."

I leaned against the bar top and looked at Lin and Lois. They both deadpanned their disbelief at me.

"I know how to be casual," I said. "Relax. You two are just going to call attention to us if you keep staring at me like that."

"What can I get you three?" A gruff voice came from behind me, and I winked at Lois and Lin before I turned around.

"Holy crap," I all but shouted when I laid eyes on the bartender standing behind the bar. "Are you Santa?"

The whole establishment went quiet, and all eyes went to us again.

"Way to go, Subtle Sally," Lois whispered, then leaned away from me.

The bartender had a glass in his hand and had been toweling it off before my blaring question. Now he glared at me, unmoving as he sneered past his corn cob pipe. "You in here to make trouble? Because if you want trouble, I'll serve all you can eat."

"No, sir."

I stared at him unblinking, trying to rectify what I saw, with what I knew. The bartender was a portly satyr, half man, half goat, but instead of having brown fur on his bottom half, it was fire engine red. I caught a glimpse of jet-black hooves and he wore no shirt in true satyr fashion. His torso was covered in tattoos and he had a long white beard. Add to that his corncob pipe and gold circular glasses and he was the spitting image of old St. Nick ... minus the goat legs of course. Put a big red coat on him and a hat to cover the short black horns protruding from his forehead, and he'd be ready to jump into a sleigh and drive eight tiny reindeer.

"Please forgive me. We're from ... out of town. You just reminded me of someone I knew once."

When the bartender didn't try to bash my head in, the patrons got bored and went back to their conversations. I wished I could say as much for our less than jolly host.

"You don't say." He went back to drying his glass and leaned in my direction. "You know I did a tour on your planet. Worst deployment I ever had in the service. I was attacked by animals, shot more times than I can count, one guy even tried to trap me in a cage. Can you believe that? I wouldn't go back to Earth for all the credits in the universe."

I stared with my mouth half open not knowing what to say.

"Can I just get a glass of water?" Lois leaned around me and closed my jaw with her fingers.

Santa nodded.

"I would like a sparkling Alerian nectar please," Lin added.

The bartender's eyes sparkled a little when he realized a Peeri hid beneath Lin's deep hood. Then I looked again, and I wasn't sure if they sparkled or if it was a trick of the light against his square pupils.

"And what about you, Slick?" He turned those shining eyes on me. "What do you want?"

I paused for half a moment longer, regaining my bearings, then smiled. "I'm Ben. Do you have a special or something?"

I heard Lin, Buttercup and even Lois groan in unison. I ignored their protest and pressed on. After all, the way to anyone's heart is by expressing interest in the thing they love. This guy was a bartender. I wanted to see what he could do.

"I'll bet you have a drink you're the best at, Mr. ..." I left the sentence hanging hoping he would fill in his name.

He stared at me for a moment then grinned. "Nicolao. Stellish Nicolao."

He held out a hand and I shook it.

"Folks around here call me—"

"Let me guess." Before I could finish, Lois slapped her hand to my mouth.

"Why don't you just let the nice gentleman tell us his name?"

"Folks around here call me Stella."

I snorted. Then caught myself as Lois tentatively pulled her hand away. "Stella. Cool name. That's what I was going to guess for sure."

Stella eyed me for a moment, then went on making our drinks. He poured Lois's water, lame, then made Lin's fancy nectar, which didn't look too bad. Then it was my turn.

He pulled out an insulated metal highball glass from under the bar and slammed it down on top, then proceeded to pour three glowing liquids into the cup. When the first two mixed, the glass frosted over. The third caused the glass to began to sweat and steam. Then he pulled out an eyedropper and ever so carefully, from a full arm's length away, let a single drop of some doomsday topper fall into the glass. As soon as it hit, the whole thing spit and cracked like dropping dry ice into a hot tub.

Everyone in the bar roared with cheers and laughter, and I realized they were all watching us again. Wonderful.

"There you go." Stella's grin was now a full-on smile. He still clutched his corncob pipe in the teeth, but I could tell he was barely able to hold it together. "I call it, Stranger Danger."

I looked at the glass. "So, is this more of a sipping kind of thing or—"

"All in one go. You might want to hurry. I don't know how long that cup is going to last."

I touched the metal surface and it felt cold and warm in different places.

"You have to drink it," Buttercup said. "You do not order

the bartender's special in a place like this then turn it down. It is an insult. And no matter what you think of it, don't show anything but delicious satisfaction if you want any information. I have analyzed the ingredients. They will not kill you in this configuration, though they will produce some interesting sensations on their way back out. We can discuss that later."

I nodded. "Okay. Can't wait to try it." I stared at the glass working up my nerve. The bar was so silent they could probably hear my heart beating in my chest. How could it get any worse than this?

I picked up the glass and downed the whole thing in one shot, swallowing as hard and fast as I could. The bar erupted in cheers, and I stopped breathing.

TWENTY-FIVE

I did my best to smile and set the glass down on the bar. My taste buds all seemed to stand up and scream at the same time, somehow sensing a strange mix of strawberries, gasoline and stale pickle relish with just a dash of teargas as a garnish. Inside, it didn't feel like my stomach was burning, but rather that all of my organs had been filled with molten magnesium and they were about to melt their way out of my pelvis and run into my boots. I felt my face go red as sweat poured down my forehead. All the while Stella kept smiling and watching.

"Are you okay?" Lois squeezed in beside me and waved a hand in front of my face, but my eyes were fixed on Stella.

"Wait for it," he said, holding up a finger. Then, when I could hold my breath no longer, I let out a long wheezing gasp. Ice-cold air heaved out of my mouth and nose releasing a huge cloud of vapor. I felt frost form on my lips and the burning sensation was gone, leaving behind a freezing cold so deep in my core it made me shiver.

Another cheer rose from the bar, and I clutched my stomach more out of shock than pain.

"That was horrible." The words were out of my mouth before I knew I had said them.

Lois smacked my arm, and I looked up to see Stella's smile turned to a frown. His pipe went limp in his teeth, and he stopped drying his glass to glare at me.

"Enjoy your stay here. Finish your drinks and get out. And don't forget to pay. Like it or not, Stranger Danger ain't cheap."

He started to walk away, and I forced myself to stand straight again, our chance for information slipping away.

"Wait." I held up a hand. "Please come back. Let me apologize."

Stella turned ever so slowly, and I beckoned him in. I couldn't let the opportunity go to waste. Not after enduring the torture of Stranger Danger. Stella faced me at the bar and finished drying his glass, before setting it down.

"Ok?"

I hauled off and slapped him.

The bar went dead silent for about three heartbeats, then everyone broke into raucous laughter. Everyone but Stella. He reached under the bar and pulled out a gun.

My eyes went wide.

"I suppose this is as good a place as any to start looking for a new captain." Buttercup's voice rang out in my head, but I was too busy trying not to die. Stella took aim at my head and I ducked, but I was only three feet away. He really couldn't miss.

"Wait, Sir." Lin jumped in between us and stuck his finger in the barrel of the gun. Never in my life, other than in a cartoon, had I seen someone do that. Apparently, it caught Stella off guard as well.

"Don't do that." Stella tried to pull away, but they were too close, and Lin had a long arm.

"You know what they say about humans." Lin leaned

forward and whispered something only Stella could hear. Lois and I looked at each other, then Stella leaned back and laughed.

"Yeah, I suppose you're right."

Lin pulled his finger out of the barrel and Stella stowed it under his bar. "You two better be careful around here. This is not the place for a couple of Atavistics. Folks around here would as soon blast you as look at you."

I resisted the urge to ask what an atavistic was, or to mention he was about to blast me three seconds ago.

"Unfortunately, we don't have much choice," I said. "We're looking for someone. He goes by the name Olamer. He's looking to traffic some new merchandise, real new, and we need to know where to find him."

Stella picked up his glass and started toweling it off again even though it was dry.

"New merchandise is one way to put it." Stella sneered. "I don't inform on my clients. It's bad for business, but I heard him talking and I don't allow anyone to traffic kids. Especially a baby. Not of any race. Life is tough enough without getting a start like that." Stella kept his voice low so only we could hear him.

He eyed a couple of tall aqua-skinned patrons standing nearby and nodded off to the right.

"Why don't you two enjoy your drinks somewhere else?"

"What?" the one closest to us said. "Where?"

"I don't care where, just beat it." Stella stared them down and I thought he might be goat enough to take on the Bane I bumped into outside ... even if the Bane brought a few of his friends.

The aqua aliens stumbled away and Stella turned his attention to us again. "I kicked Olamer out of my joint a few hours ago. He was in the back corner talking to one of those Scavid slime bags. I don't usually serve those bio-haters either. As soon as I heard Olamer was looking to make a deal with them, I made it my business to find out what the deal was for. I can't have the Scavid getting their hands on anything dangerous, especially in my bar."

If Stella only knew who, or what Bubbles was, he might have kicked them out way earlier. As it was, it sounded like Stella didn't know what Olamer had. Only that Olamer had a baby, and that was enough for him.

"As soon as I found out they were dealing kids, I booted them out on their ears. I run a respectable place. I don't need that kind of trouble."

I nodded.

"Do you have any idea where they went?" Lois asked. "We really want to get that little girl back to her parents."

Stella eyed us for another second, then nodded. "You three seem like good people, even if you are a little naive." He stared at me for a moment. "I heard they were meeting at the docks this evening. The Scavid are moored in slip 4-xeno-6. I guess they are doing the deal somewhere around there. Go get that little girl and keep her safe."

I nodded. "Thank you. We'll do our best."

Lois and Lin took one last drink, then put their glasses on the bar. "What do we owe you for the drinks?"

Stella waved us off. "They're on the house. It was worth it to see you down that Stranger Danger. Free tip, don't ever order the bartender special unless you want the baddest drink in the house."

"I will definitely remember that." I waved and we all got up to leave, but then I turned around, unable to resist.

"I have to ask, you said you did a tour on Earth. Does that

mean there are other ..." I motioned my hand toward the bright red fur on his legs.

Stella just smiled and put a finger to the side of his nose. "Go get that little girl. I'm sure she would like to see Santa's sleigh next year."

TWENTY-SIX

We made it all the way to the Xeno level without punching, slapping, bumping into, insulting, or even causing someone to want to shoot us in the face with a giant space gun. And by 'we' I mean me. On any other day I would have called that a win, but today we had more important deeds to contend with. Time ticked away too fast, and we needed to get things moving if we were going to rescue Bubbles and make it back in time to save Alma and her crew.

"This is dock four," Lin said, pointing down the walkway of a busy port loading zone. "Slot six should be ahead there at the end."

There was no question he was correct. From where we stood, I could already see the Scavid ship looming at the end of the dock. After going to war with one on earth, I would have been happy to never lay eyes on another of their mini death stars again. As it was, we were going to march right into this one's shadow and knock on the door.

The docks weren't nearly as congested as the commerce area, but it still bustled with activity. Cranes hoisted cargo, bots criss-crossed from side to side delivering crates and aliens of all kinds lumbered about their business of loading, cross checking or repairing. Sounds and smells of greasy machinery and working hydraulics permeated the stale air. Like pretty much every place we had been so far, it was amazing and over-whelming at the same time.

"We should try to stay out of sight." Lois veered to the right, ducking behind one of the many piles of crates stacked and ready for loading. "We have no idea where they are or even if they're here yet. The last thing we need is for Olamer to come strolling in behind us."

I nodded and kept pace with Lois as she wove her way through another set of crates covered in cargo nets, ready to haul away.

"Hey, Lin. I'm curious. What did you say to Stella back there that backed him off me so fast? Some sort of secret pass-word or something?"

"Not a secret password, it is an old galactic saying."

"Well let's have it." I tiptoed across another open area and slowed next to a huge tank of some kind. "Might be handy if I ever run into a situation like that again."

"I am not sure it would be appropriate ..."

"Come on," I pressed. "You said it wasn't a secret. Tell me."

Lin sighed. "Just be aware, I did not create the saying. I only used it to keep you from dying."

"Okay." Now I was getting suspicious. How bad could this be? Something about my friend from Nantucket?

"The saying goes, *wisdom is recognizing nobility, even in the actions of a half-witted Human.* Other than the literal trans-lation, it means one should be wise enough to see past the thoughtless action of someone who means well."

I blinked.

"On behalf of the human race I think I am offended and flattered all at the same time."

I started to say something else, but Lois yanked me forward by my jacket and pulled me down. "There they are."

Lin crouched beside us and I peeked over the neat stack of crates that made up our hideout. They were not metal or wood, but they were not exactly made of plastic either. If I were going to compare them to something, I would say they were like that faux-decking material that lasted longer than the house it was installed on.

I stood high enough to peer through a crack in the crates and saw Olamer facing two of the white armored Scavid analogs. The Scavid were not living beings, but computer sentients that could be transferred from place to place. They used these armored humanoid analogs to move around and interact with other species. It was like talking to an armored swat team only without the personality or trigger discipline.

"We're too late." Lois squinted through another crack in the crates. "The Scavid already have Bubbles. She must be in that box." The desperate panic percolating in her voice gave me pause. I needed to make sure she didn't do anything stupid. After all, that was my job.

I looked at them again and saw that the Scavid were indeed toting a box between the two of them. Something smallish and clear; about the right size to hold a creature like Bubbles.

"I don't think that's her." The first Scavid obscured my view, but I caught a glimpse of the contents, and it didn't look like Bubbles. "Besides if the deal was done, they would be leaving. Olamer looks like he's still negotiating—"

"Oh, that's low even for you, Olamer," Lin said, as he watched the meeting unfold. He had a slightly better angle and when the Scavid holding the box moved, he must have recognized what was inside.

"What?" I said as Lois and I both turned our eyes toward him.

"That cage contains several Parvis. A rare species who are often captured and traded on the slave market due to their size and vast skillsets."

I continued to watch the exchange. "Did you say several? That box can't be much more than twelve by twelve. How big are these Parvis?"

"Usually, six to eight inches tall. They have been horribly exploited over the centuries and almost their entire race is thought to be extinct or trapped in slavery."

I looked at the box again. "Six inches tall?"

"Creatures come in all shapes and sizes," Buttercup said in my head. "Even the intelligent ones. The Parvis are not the only micro species, and there are many who would dwarf the size of a human as well. The Viraquin, for instance, is a giant creature when it is full grown."

"Right now, I'm interested in only one creature," I said. "And, as far as I can tell, Bubbles isn't here."

I watched the Scavid hold up the clear ventilated box and Olamer shook his head, apparently not happy with the bargain being offered.

"He wouldn't have turned her over already," Lois said. "Not before the Scavid came up with their end of the deal."

I thought about it. "Buttercup. Is there a way you can scan the area to see if you can find Bubbles?"

"There are multiple life forms in the area and the array of tech present on the different space crafts is interfering with my ability to get a clear picture, I am sorry."

"That's okay."

"You have an idea where Bubbles could be located." Lin said it as more as a statement than a question.

"Maybe." I nodded. "Think about it. If I were Olamer, here all alone, meeting with an entire Scavid ship, I wouldn't bring the merchandise to the meeting. I wouldn't even risk having it in a place where the Scavid could find it, like on my ship. If we were back on earth, I would choose a spot with lots of people and then drive there early in a rented car and park in an inconspicuous location. Hide the merchandise in the trunk or something."

"You would hide a baby in the trunk?" Lois had an expression that somehow crossed horror with disgust.

"What's a trunk?" Lin asked.

I looked at Lin and then back to Lois. "No." I pinched the bridge of my nose with my fingers. "Of course not. I'm just saying, I would get here early and hide my part of the deal until the Scavid showed proof that they were going to hold up their end of the bargain. Then I would pull mine out and make the trade."

I saw realization dawn on both of their faces, and they began to look around.

"She could be anywhere," Lin said. "There are hundreds, maybe thousands of crates and shipping containers on this dock. She could be in any one of them."

"I don't think so." I scanned the area as well. "He'd want something close by, so he could keep an eye on it. Then it would need to be moved or opened by hand, so these huge crates are out." I motioned to the big industrial sized boxes in front of us.

"And Olamer is short. He would not be reaching up for something seven feet above the ground," Lois said, catching on. "He'd choose something low and probably heavy because he is strong. He wouldn't want just anyone to be able to trip over her by accident."

"Over there." Lin motioned to a stack of crates about fifty yards away. At first, I didn't see what he was looking at. They were just as large as the crates we were hiding behind. Big enough for a crane or forklift to move. Then I saw what he was talking about. A stack of smaller boxes on the far corner, and they weren't piled quite right. Almost as if they had been knocked over and then reshuffled in place again without taking the time to really pack them in.

I peeked through the crack and saw Olamer shaking his head at the Scavid. "We better hurry before the Scavid meets his price." The three of us scampered forward, taking turns weaving our way through the cargo and supplies. We were much closer to Olamer and the Scavid now. Close enough to hear their conversation. Olamer would have his one eye on the crates to be sure his prize didn't walk away. We would have to take care not to be seen.

We all crouched on the far side of the pile Lin had spotted. Fortunately, the smaller boxes were located on the side opposite Olamer's location. He faced us, but as long as we stayed low, he wouldn't see us.

Lois reached out to move the closest box and managed to do nothing but turn her face beat red.

"We're never going to be able to move these things," she whispered.

"No deal." I heard Olamer say. "I will have all five or you can find your item elsewhere. You won't find another like mine anywhere in the universe, I can tell you that."

I ground my teeth and resisted the urge to throw the closest rock at Olamer's head. How could anyone trade away lives so easily? If there were a true evil in the universe, it was the slave trader.

I motioned for Lois to move out of the way, and I looked in between the crack of the stacked boxes. Sure enough, there was a void, though I wasn't sure if anything was inside. Only one way to find out.

I sat on the ground and braced my feet against the crates and pushed ... and the only thing that moved was me.

"What the heck is in these things? And how strong is Olamer?"

"Perhaps if we all worked together," Lin said, scooching his way over so he could get a hand on the crates as well.

I nodded. "One ..."

Lois moved in and got her feet against the crate and so did I.

"Two ... three."

We all heaved, and the crates scraped along the ground with a loud groan. We all froze.

I listened for Olamer or the Scavid. Neither said a word. If they heard us, we were sitting ducks out here in the open. I didn't even have my revolver because Buttercup said they would have confiscated it when we went into the bar.

Seconds ticked by like hours before I heard Olamer's voice again. "All or nothing. Take it or leave it."

My shoulders relaxed and we all moved. I glanced around to the corner to see Olamer and the Scavid still standing where they should be. Lois reached into the hollow and pulled out a bundle of blankets. When she unwrapped them, I almost laughed with relief. Tears came to my eyes as I looked at a slumbering little Viraquin in Lois's arms.

"She's asleep, but I think she's okay." Lois stroked Bubble's smooth head blinking back her own tears of relief and joy.

Seeing Bubbles filled me with hope, but I would not be truly happy until her bright eyes were open, and she was alight with the cheer we were accustomed to seeing pulse along her skin.

"Let's get out of here," Lois said, dropping the excess blankets to the ground.

"Wait." I wiped away my tears and grabbed the spare blankets, balling them into a knot roughly the size of a bowling ball. Lois still had one to cover Bubbles, but the extra's might act as enough of a decoy to give us a few extra seconds. Who knows, maybe Olamer will bring the empty bundle all the way over to the Scavid and open it right in front of them. I would love to be there to see that. I knew from experience, the Scavid did not like it when they were double-crossed.

"Okay." I pointed back the way we came. "Let's go before they find us."

Lin led the way, followed by Lois then me. We wove our way from one stack of crates to the next, taking care not to be spotted by either Olamer or the Scavid. I hated even being near their ship for fear they might look down and see us scurrying around. We were just about past them and ready to make a run for the end of the dock, when two more Scavid caught my eye. These were not the two who were dealing with Olamer, but a new pair, and they were walking down the dock dragging a third individual with them.

My heart sank as they marched by, kicking and prodding their prisoner forward. It was Stella. He looked bruised and beaten and limped heavily on his right leg. I didn't know why they had him here, but if they dragged him all the way from the Black Star, I had a feeling the message meant bad news for Bubbles and her ragtag rescue crew.

TWENTY-SEVEN

"What are we going to do?" Lois crouched low with Lin. Through a void in a large pile of cargo nets we could see Stella and his captors coming up on Olamer and the other two Scavid.

Part of me wanted to keep moving. A big part. If I'm being honest, ninety-nine percent. We needed to protect Bubbles. She was the one they were all looking for. We were her only defenders. If we were caught or killed, she would be defenseless and on her own. There would be nothing we could do to stop all the Scavids and Olamers of the universe from exploiting Bubbles for her powers.

On the other hand, there was that one percent. That tiny part that said we could not leave Stella to the Scavid. He helped us. I don't know if I would call him a friend, but he didn't deserve to be left all alone either.

We looked on as the captors dropped Stella at the other two Scavid's feet. We had worked our way up the dock toward our escape, but our route had kept us closer to the Scavid ship than we were on the way in, so we could hear their angry shouts.

"Establishment Proprietor reports human, Ben, in vicinity. Human, Ben, destruct priority."

"I told you no such thing you dirty gearbox." Stella spat at the ground. "You pulled the information out of my head with that brain melter you carry around. If you didn't have that, I would have torn you both into scrap."

"The Scavid know you?" Lin furrowed his brow at me, looking both shocked and a little impressed.

"Yeah," I whispered. "Lois, Buttercup and I sort of destroyed one of their ships. That's how we wound up babysitting this little bundle. The Scavid were after her mother. They couldn't get her, so now it seems they've switched their sights to Bubbles."

Lin nodded. "I mean no offense by this whatsoever, and I hope you are not bothered by me stating the obvious, but you are all going to die."

Lois and I blinked at Lin.

"Of course not. Why would we be bothered by a statement like that?" I scoffed.

"Don't get me wrong. You are obviously a formidable enemy. That, or you are incredibly lucky. But the Scavid do not forget such transgressions. They will hunt you down, even if there is only one Scavid left in the entire universe. They are known for their long, detailed memories. The downside to an artificial intelligence is that old wounds do not fade with time. An offense is just as vivid in twenty years as the moment it happened. They will never forget about any of you ... ever."

"Well, thanks captain optimism," I said. "We have done all right so far. I'm sure we will figure things out as we go along."

"Yes, well, perhaps we should conclude our business as soon as possible. The Peeri do not like to have an unsettled debt on the books, even if the proprietors of the contract are dead."

"I get the picture," I snapped as I turned my attention to Olamer and the Scavid again. "You are not a fan. Don't worry. I don't plan on dying anytime soon."

Our discussion had distracted us all from seeing what was happening near the Scavid ship. Now that I was watching again, I saw Olamer return from a pile of crates with an arm full of blankets. The same blankets I had balled up and stuffed into his hiding spot a few moments earlier.

"The infant is gone," Olamer bellowed. "You and your creaky scarecrows have wasted all my time and now I have nothing to show for it. This is your fault. The infant was here for the deal. You delayed and now your prize is gone. It is up to you to find it. I want my five Parvis in payment as promised. The infant is your problem now."

Olamer reached for the cage, but the Scavid pulled back. "Negative. No infant, no Parvis. Provide infant."

That last part sounded like more of a threat than a request. The four Scavid surrounded Olamer, and left Stella largely forgotten at their feet.

"You lost her," Olamer said, then reached forward and grabbed the handle on top of the cage. "You find her."

He produced a hidden weapon from up his sleeve and blasted the Scavid holding the Parvis cage. The Scavid flew backward, jerking the box and Olamer lost his grip as well. The cage sailed through the air and landed on the dock, sliding a good twenty yards before coming to a halt ten feet away from where we hid.

Olamer tracked his prize for a moment, but he had bigger things to worry about. The other three Scavid moved in, drawing weapons out of hidden compartments on their thighs. The two behind him would have turned his head into a canoe had it not been for Stella. He rose and bare-fisted one in the head then came around and elbowed the other in the neck. He hit them both so hard it threw them off balance, giving Olamer enough time to turn and get two more shots off.

That should have been Stella's cue to run, but instead he tackled the last Scavid to the ground before it could bring its own blaster to bear against either one of them.

"Okay, we should probably go." I reached out and took Bubbles out of Lois's arms. "I think Olamer and Stella are going to be fine. That or they're going to wind up fighting an entire Scavid army. Either way we need to get out of—"

Before I could finish, I saw another Scavid rounding on their position. It came up on their blind side so neither of them had spotted it. The compartment on the Scavid's thigh opened and it drew a blaster, moving silent and deadly. There was no way they would see him in time.

My eyes went wild, not knowing what to do. I had Bubbles in my arm so I couldn't run into the fray. Yelling wouldn't do any good either. The Scavid would still get the shot off. I looked everywhere for a solution. Then I found it. A three-pound sledgehammer sitting on the crate to my right. I grabbed the hammer without thinking and hurled it at the Scavid. There was no time to take aim, and I was far from an athletic super-star, but I chucked it with everything I had. The heavy projec-tile twirled through the air in a perfect low arc, tumbling silently end over end. For a moment I thought the hammer would fly high, missing the Scavid's head by inches, then it dipped at the last second and slammed into the Scavid's skull. Its head jerked over at an angle that would have killed a human, but it only seemed to knock the Scavid off balance, causing him to stumble for a moment.

"Watch out!" Olamer and Stella looked to me, then to the Scavid who was trying to recover and blindside them. Olamer blasted him before he could take another shot, but the damage had been done.

"Human Ben identified."

The Scavid on the ground grappling with Stella pointed at me and made his declaration at full volume, no doubt notifying the other Scavid who were responding from the ship. Stella pounded it in the head with his fist three times then twisted his armored skull around until the blue lights in its eyes went out with a loud metallic crunch. Olamer and Stella both looked to me again, then to the bundle in my arms.

"That's mine," Olamer screamed. He started to run at me, but he didn't get far. Four more Scavid appeared from beneath the huge spherical ship, charging him before he could give chase.

"Get out of here you crazy Vistics." Stella looked barbarous as he untangled himself from the mangled Scavid at his feet. He pointed at us, then back up the dock toward our escape. "We'll take care of these bio-haters. Olamer and I can work things out after that."

I stared at him for another second.

"Go," he shouted, then charged in to fight another Scavid coming off the ship.

Lois, Lin and I all turned to follow his order. I didn't know if I would see Stella again, but I owed him more than a drink if I ever did. He helped us find Bubbles and now he risked his life to save us. I don't care what anyone thought, he was the baddest Santa who ever lived. But for now, we just had to run.

TWENTY-EIGHT

"How much time do we have?" I set Bubbles on my captain's chair and carefully peeled away the blankets. Twitch was with me, peeling them back as well, eager to see his friend again.

"We will cross the stations warp dampening line in a few minutes." Buttercup answered over the ship's speakers. "I am charging the Warpstream Generators now. As long as we don't run into any delays, we should have just enough time to return to the Peeri ship."

"Excellent." I pulled off the last layer of blanket as Lois peered over my shoulder. Even Lin had come over to check on our little rescue. He stood across from me looking down his nose at Bubbles.

I could not help but smile when I saw her. The bioluminescent light played across her skin in slow gentle waves and her big blue eyes were closed, but she was alive and seemed to be well.

"Hey." I reached out to touch her head. "Bubbles. Wake up. You're safe now. It's us."

I waited a second, then jostled her gently, making her tiny little tentacles wiggle. Her little mouth hung slack, and she did not respond. Twitch poked her cheek with his hand a little harder than he probably should have and let out a chitter of his own.

"Easy there, buddy," I said.

Worry spread through me as I looked at Lois. "Something's wrong. Do you think Olamer drugged her?"

Lois shrugged. "Maybe. He stunned her while he was here and that knocked her out."

She reached town and touched her head. "She feels a little warm, but really, I have no idea. He must have done something to keep her from folding away, but I have no way of knowing what that could be. She's an alien. For all we know, caffeine could render her unconscious."

I ground my teeth in frustration and fury. I was glad Bubbles was in one piece, but so help me, if she did not come out of this okay, I would circle back and—

"Perhaps we could be of some assistance."

A strange voice came from my right, but when I turned to look there was no one there.

"Don't be angry." Lois blurted out before I could say anything.

"Be angry about what?" I still searched for the origin of the voice when my gaze went down to the deck. There on the icy looking floor, stood five miniature ... I wasn't sure what they were. They had the short stocky build of a gnome, but none of them wore the weird pointy hats or long white beards. Their clothing had more of a steampunk feel, with armored shoulder pads, gloves and circular goggles. They all seemed to be laden with wearable tech of one kind or another, but none of it seemed dangerous. Instead, they looked more like tiny, walking, multi-tools, ready to tackle any job or challenge set before them. Each was color coordinated as well. The one speaking had bright red hair and mostly red clothing and gear. He seemed to specialize in medical skills as he had a stethoscope draped below his scruffy red beard and telescopic goggles that seemed tailored for close magnification and examinations."

"Wha ... how did ..." I gestured toward our tiny new guests.

"I couldn't just leave them there," Lois said. "Olamer would have traded them into slavery. If not him, someone would have grabbed them. You heard what Lin said about their people. While you played Thor with your hammer, I snuck over and snatched the cage. It was the perfect distraction."

She looked at Lin as if for confirmation. He just raised an eyebrow. Whether he was in disbelief or agreement I wasn't sure.

"Oh, come on." Lois knelt next to the group of Parvis huddled together on the floor. "Lin said they're handy. Maybe they can help. I'm a biologist and you are a nurse and neither of us has any idea how to help Bubbles."

Despite their size and situation, they did not look weak or scared. I had to admire their fortitude if nothing else. All they seemed to want was a job. A way to help and keep their hands busy. No wonder they were so highly prized on the slave market.

"I can't believe this." I backed off just enough to allow the Parvis access to Bubbles on the chair. "We're turning into an alien orphanage. Go ahead, but if you do anything to hurt her ... "

I glared at the little group of responders. They didn't even flinch. I was about to reach down and help them all up to the seat, but they all ran forward and made a sort of living ladder, climbing up over one another, then hauling the bottom ones up as they went. They moved together as a cohesive, practiced, well-oiled machine.

One of the Parvis dressed in yellow leather, with bright yellow hair, stopped to peer at me through a pair of glowing goggles. One lens was a golden yellow, while the other jutted out in a telescopic copper housing hiding both of her eyes.

"I'm Jib. The one in Purple is Molly, Green is Heshel, Blue is Dash and the medic in Red is Frig. He's very good at what he does. One of the best. Your friend will be okay, I promise."

Jib did a backflip off the arm of the chair and joined her four other compatriots while Twitch watched over them. He was two or three inches taller than the Parvis and looked like a towering monster in comparison. He growled and whined, not quite sure what to do as they poked and prodded, soothed and healed.

"It's alright little guy." I reached down and let him run up my arm. He seemed relieved at the opportunity to retreat. "They're trying to help."

Lois put a hand on my shoulder and even Lin seemed apprehensive as we watched.

Frig did most of the work, though the others assisted, pulling out one strange monitor, then the next. The instruments seemed somehow archaic and incredibly advanced at the same time. He muttered something I couldn't hear, then I noticed they all became uneasy, casting the three of us sidelong glances as Frig pulled something out of a side pocket on his backpack and handed it to Dash, the blue Parvis standing across from him. He was small so it was hard to see what he was doing, but I could tell they were purposely hiding this from our view.

"Hold on," I said. "Reaching in to grab Frig's little arm. "What's that?"

Molly and Heshel, the purple and green Parvis jumped in my way, waving their arms up at me in distraction and blocking me from Frig. "Don't worry. Frig knows what he's doing. Your friend is in—"

I reached past them, but Frig already had some kind of pads hooked to either side of Bubbles' head where her temples might be. They reminded me of an EKG or miniature defibrillator pads. When I heard a whine then a crack of electricity, I knew which one it was.

My own heart stopped. Did Frig just send a jolt of electricity into Bubbles' brain?

I was about to snatch the little red Parvis right off the chair when Bubbles' eyes began to flitter open.

Relief surged through me as I jerked the tiny electrodes off her head and pulled Bubbles into my arms. "What did you do to her?"

Lois reached out to stroke her head. "Ben, I think she is okay."

Bubbles peered at me with sleepy eyes.

Frig had his hands up in a placating gesture. The wires and electrodes still hung out of the side of his backpack and none of them made any effort to pack them away again.

"I'm sorry." Frig's voice was squeaky like a cartoon and gruff at the same time. "Your little friend was in real trouble. If I had stopped to explain, it might have been too late."

"Too late?" I gripped Bubbles a little tighter.

"Yes. Her voltaic system was in crisis due to what may have been a stun charge or a severe electrical shock. This creature is incredibly sensitive to electrical fields. At least right now. She may grow out of it, but if I had not reset her system, she would have died within moments. You're lucky I was here."

I peered at Bubbles, and she snuggled into my arm, seeming

to sigh with relief. The bioluminescent light along her skin flashed and waved in a way I recognized. Her mother had flashed her lights in the same way to communicate with us.

"Did she just say something?" I looked at the viewscreen at the front of the ship. Buttercup had repaired almost all the damage Olamer had done to the bridge and only a few long cracks on the screen remained.

"Yes, I believe she said, Thank Ben, Thank Lois, Thank tiny."

"Wow." I smiled at Bubbles. "You're welcome. Maybe you should get some rest. You're safe now."

I glanced at Frig for confirmation and he nodded once.

"Thank you. I don't know what I would have done if ..." I couldn't even bring myself to finish the sentence.

"I believe these creatures have earned passage on your vessel." Lin eyed me with that no nonsense expression that said this was a Peeri understanding and would not be refused. A favor for a favor. That's how their society worked and there was no wiggle room around it.

"Of course, they have earned passage. They would have been welcome even if they hadn't saved Bubbles."

I looked at the crew of heroes. "But I'm glad you did."

Lin responded with a cynical humph, but didn't say anything else.

"So am I," Lois said. "Thank you so much for helping her. We had no idea she was so injured."

Frig gathered his wires and electrodes, coiled them carefully then stowed them in his bag.

"The condition is unusual and not many would have recognized it." Frig sounded almost like he was bragging, but his voice held no arrogance or malice. He just stated a fact. "I'm glad we were here to help."

"We will be ready to activate the Warpstream in ten seconds," Buttercup announced.

"Maybe we should all take our seats." I looked around, wondering what to do with the Parvis now that we had no more space for passengers.

"They can ride with me," Lois said. "As long as you don't mind doubling up in my chair."

Frig nodded his head. "We would be honored to ride with our liberator."

Lin sat in his chair, and I took my seat, holding Bubbles. We all watched the screen, ready to see the light show, then Buttercup counted down.

"Three ... two ... one."

Nothing happened. I heard the Warpstream Generator whine up to activate, but we didn't move. Then an alarm went off on the bridge.

"Incoming ship." Buttercup's voice turned frantic. "Scavid attack class. They are using a warp dampener to prevent us from escaping. Taking evasive action."

TWENTY-NINE

Buttercup switched to Battlesight mode giving us a nearly three-sixty view of the area around us. I laid Bubbles, now asleep, onto my lap. I saw the weapon screens pop up in front of Lois out of the corner of my eye, and to their credit, the Parvis seemed to take all of this in stride. All five of them climbed up to the back of Lois's chair to sit high and out of the way.

Buttercup pulled up hard and the inertia dampeners took much of the force, making our sudden direction change feel less jarring than it looked on screen. The Scavid ship came into view almost immediately and opened fire with its energy cannons.

Bolts of bright red light streaked through space, overshooting our position. More cannons appeared as door after door irised open on the Scavid's orbital hull. Red light came down on us like rain and Buttercup dodged and weaved through it all, barrel-rolling, banking and looping around the less agile Scavid ship.

"Bring us around to face her," I shouted. "Maybe we can

get a shot off to distract them, then we can get away."

Buttercup managed another spectacular loop and brought us in, right on top of the Scavid's dome.

"Lois." I pointed at her without looking. "Rail gun and energy cannon. Try to target some of those open gun hatches."

Lois let go with a barrage of fire. Green bolts bounced off the Scavid's hull, but I thought at least one of the railgun shots may have gotten past their defenses.

I saw one of the gun hatches emitting smoke and sparks, but we were repaid with a hit from their energy cannons as well. Buttercup jolted and shook as our shields took most of the impact, but a heads-up image appeared in front of me annotating the shield location and percentage.

Currently, our rearward radiating energy shields were operating at forty percent. Not good.

"The Scavid defenses are holding," Buttercup reported. "Energy cannons had minimal effect."

"We hit something with the rail gun," I exclaimed.

"An unlikely shot and it did no real damage. They have fifty of those energy cannons. If we take a hit like that every time we go to destroy one, we will be killed on the third round."

"I really hate these guys." I turned to Lois. "What about Skipper missiles or rocket drones?"

"They refitted us while we were in port at Fafnir," Buttercup answered. "But Skipper missiles will have no offensive effect on the Scavid's defensive systems."

Skipper missiles worked with a mini warp engine allowing them to skip through space and fool energized directional shielding systems like the one Buttercup had. The Scavid had devised an energized hull that required no directional or high energy outer shield. Their defenses were up all the time, at every angle, making a Skipper missile all but useless against them.

"Fire the rocket drones then!" I shouted. "At least that might throw them off. All we need is a little time to get away."

Lois launched a battery of twelve drones and the Scavid responded with immediate counter measures I hadn't seen before. A green cloud jetted from the Scavid ship, changing direction and gaining speed as if it were a solid object. It enveloped eight of the drones and sent them reeling off course the moment the cloud made contact. The drones spiraled and sputtered, crashing into one another, or just flittered uselessly into space.

The other four stayed on target however and latched onto the Scavid hull, engaging their disruptive rockets, and sending the Scavid propulsion systems off course.

"Go now!" I shouted. "We might not get another chance."

Buttercup leveled out and sped away at full power to outrun the Scavid's warp dampening field. They fired their energy cannons, but the rocket drones threw their targeting systems off as well, spinning and tilting their ship in random directions.

"This is going to work. How far do we have to get?"

"Far," Buttercup responded. "Their dampening beam is locked onto my hull and has an impressive range. I am not sure how far we will have to go in order to outrun it."

"Keep going," I said. "We can make it."

"What are those?" Lin pointed to another heads-up display to my left. It showed a green triangle, a red circle and several red dots in-between that seemed to be gaining on the triangle.

"Those are missiles." Buttercup's voice was grave and emotionless. "The Scavid have a lock for those as well."

"What?" I turned to Lois. "How many?"

She shook her head. "Four, no six."

"Are we going to make it? Can we jump into the Warp-stream before they get here?"

"Calculating." Buttercup's impassive statement hung in the air for several seconds, then. "Negative. We will not outrun their dampening field before the missiles make contact."

"Fine," I said. "Turn and face them. We'll shoot the missiles down."

"If I alter course or power, they will impact before we can react."

"What then?" I threw up my hands. "We just wait to die?"

"Incoming ship detected. Arges class." Buttercup paused and this time even her voice betrayed our bleak reality. "It is the Crooked Foot. Olamer's ship is on an intercept course from our starboard side."

I stared at the screen, trying to come up with a plan. We couldn't turn, we couldn't run, we couldn't fight, and now Olamer had us hemmed in, just in case we managed a Hail Mary to get away. We had been in some tight spots, but this one might be too small for a gnat to wiggle out of.

I looked at Lois. She had tears in her eyes as her hands hovered over the weapons display screens.

"It's okay." I offered her a weak but understanding smile. "It's not your fault. There's nothing left for us to do."

I turned around in my seat to peer at Lin. He sat in his chair upright and proper as always, looking not at all bothered by the fact that we were all about to die.

"I'm sorry we couldn't make good on that agreement. I guess you were right about the Scavid. They caught up to us sooner than later."

"It was a valiant attempt. If I am to die, I am proud to do it in your service. You are a good human, though I must confess I have only ever known two."

I snorted out a laugh. "Thanks. You are a good Peeri too. I think you've gotten a pretty bad rap for what it's worth."

Lin nodded. "Thank you."

"We have an incoming transmission from the Crooked Foot." Buttercup blurted the words out fast and breathless.

"Olamer wants to gloat." I huffed. "No thank you."

"I think you'll want to see this."

A square popup in the middle of our Battlesight appeared and not Olamer, but Stella materialized on the screen.

"Didn't I tell you Vistics to get out of here?"

I rose from my chair, nearly toppling Bubbles onto the floor. Once I fumbled her onto my seat, I stared at the screen. "We tried but the Scavid ... how did you ..."

"Olamer and I came to an understanding. He's probably waking up from that understanding about now. Why don't you take your delicate little ship away from here so the big boys can fight."

I looked over as the Crooked Foot came into view on screen and launched spiraling countermeasures at our pursuing missiles. The red dots went out one by one and then just like that, we were free of the Scavid's attack.

"Are you going to be okay? Maybe we should stay and ..."

"I said get out of here!" Stella bellowed. "I can't have you getting in my way. If we ever meet again, you owe me a drink. Now beat it before the Scavid get close enough to lock on and dampen your Warpstream again."

"Thank you." I raised a hand in farewell and looked back to see Lin and Lois were both on their feet as well. "I hope we meet again soon."

"Not me." Lois smiled. "You're nothing but trouble."

He winked, laid his finger aside his nose, then the transmission cut out and the Crooked Foot altered course to intercept the Scavid.

"With your permission," Buttercup said. "I will power up the Warpstream Generator and get us underway."

I peered out at Stella's retreating ship. "Maybe we should watch and be sure—"

"Permission granted." Buttercup engaged the drive and away we went into the nebulous stream of lights.

I hated to leave Stella alone, but he seemed determined to face the Scavid on his own and in truth, there wasn't much we could do. We were outmatched and had our own problems to worry about. The Peeri were still out there. If we didn't get back to Alma and her crew soon, they were all going to die.

I looked over at Lin and fixed my gaze on him.

"What's a Vistic? Stella keeps calling us that. What does it mean?"

Buttercup let out a snort of laughter, but Lin never lost his straight face.

"Atavistic. Ironically it is an earth word that means naive, underdeveloped, or uncivilized. Though I believe he meant it in a more affectionate connotation, most use the term in a derogatory fashion."

I nodded. "Considering how many times he pulled our bacon out of the fire, I'll give him that one. Hopefully we'll make it to your ship and prove we aren't as simple as the universe seems to think we are."

THIRTY

"They aren't responding to my hails." Buttercup spoke over the ship's speakers. Lin and I stood in the airlock with the five Parvis waiting to board the Peeri ship. Lois stayed back on the bridge with Bubbles to keep her from folding if she woke up from her nap and realized she was all alone. Twitch came with me this time, riding on my shoulder to keep me company and lend a hand if he could.

"Don't worry about it." I checked the indicator light that told us if we were clear to enter, but it was still red. "Did you manage to get life support going again?"

"Yes, but there is no way of knowing how long they have been without it. We are now powering their ship with our auxiliary batteries until the power couplings are repaired."

I looked at the Parvis. "And you're sure you know how to replace the couplings?"

Molly, the purple Parvis laughed. "We could do it with our eyes closed. We'll repair any other systems that need attention as well. Just give us a few hours and we'll have the ship running at one hundred and ten percent."

I nodded. "Alright. Medics and engineers too. The Parvis should unionize. You would make a killing."

"I don't know what that means." Dash smiled at me and tied her long, blue hair into a tiny ponytail. "We just like helping out where we can."

I chuckled and the light turned green, then I hit the panel to open the airlock door. The Peeri side of the dock remained sealed, but Lin made short work of it, and within a few seconds we stood on the deck of the Peeri cargo hold. Rotting remnants of the festivities were splattered on the floor, walls and even the ceiling. Paper streamers, plastic food dispenser packets, cups and empty alcohol pouches lay everywhere. It looked more like a dump than the loading dock for an advanced space-faring species.

"We're too late." Lin's voice was full of horror and regret. "This is all my fault."

I was about to tell him we did everything we could when a familiar voice greeted us from the passageway in the ship.

"Well, hello." Alma wandered into the cargo hold, staggering as if she'd had far too much to drink. "I thought I heard voices coming from in here." I caught Alma as she tripped into me and laughed. "I began to wonder if you were ever going to make it back to the party."

"Party?" I helped her regain her balance and then took half a step back. "How long have you been without life support? Where's the rest of your crew?"

Alma waved a hand behind her. "They're all back to work around the ship somewhere. I wasn't aware the life-support was down. I am happy you came back though."

She smiled, unbothered by the fact that she and all her crew were all mere moments from death.

I looked at Lin and he shook his head in disbelief.

"These Parvis say they can fix your ship. Do you have any objection to them examining your power coupling and communications system?" I motioned to our five temporary crew members.

"Yes of course. I will have someone bring the necessary tools. I assume you obtained the components?"

I nodded. "We did. Some Scavid gave us a little trouble but—"

"Wonderful." Alma turned and waved us forward. "We can be underway in a few hours. Shall we retire to my bridge where we can contact Lillora command? As soon as long-range communication is operable, I suggest we brief them and update our status. I am sure King Janus will be ever so happy to hear from *you*."

Her eyes went to Lin and I could not tell if Alma was serious or being facetious.

"I would very much like to tell him of your heroic efforts to save our crew."

"And what of my efforts to hamper your mission?"

Alma huffed out a laugh and waved away the accusation. "You were only doing what you thought was right. What any good Peeri would do. We should allow bygones to be bygones and get on with the matter at hand."

"And that matter would be ..." I let the statement hang.

"Why, bringing the secret of happiness to my people. That is the only true mission for us all, isn't it? To find happiness and share it with others? I have found it, and now I wish to share my discovery with all the Peeri people."

"Don't you think you're overdoing the happy a little bit?" I squinted and pinched my fingers together. "I hope you don't mind me saying so, but your ship is in shambles. If Lin is any example of how your people usually conduct themselves, I don't know if the king is going to be happy about this place."

"Nonsense," She huffed. "Once he shares in my secret, he will understand. They all will."

That's what I was afraid of. I hated to admit it, but maybe Lin had been right all along. Maybe this was a little more than the Peeri were equipped to handle. We needed to contact Lillora command alright. We would tell the king about everything that happened here, including Alma's conduct and the problems with her ship and crew. They were, after all, still Peeri, and the Peeri government should be the ones to decide how to handle things from here.

I crouched down to Frig and the others so only they could hear what I said.

"Can you five fix the ship without restoring their communications? I think we should make our own call from Buttercup and let them know what's happening from there."

Frig nodded. "No problem. We will get life-support and propulsion running and leave comms down for now."

One of Alma's crew staggered into the bay, and she addressed him with a casual wave.

"Take these five to the engine room and carry their supplies. They're going to help us get back to Lillora."

"Yes ma'am." He stepped forward and took the bucket I held in my hand containing the two power couplings, then led the five Parvis out of the room.

"Will they be okay on their own?" I asked.

"Of course," Alma slurred. "What could possibly happen to them here?"

I nodded, not at all confident about her reassurance.

"So, we held up our end of the bargain," I said, not wanting to mince words any longer. "Can we talk about that information you offered in trade?"

Alma turned to me and smiled. "Of course. The information you seek shall be provided the moment we arrive in Lillora."

"What?" I snapped. "That is not what we agreed on."

I looked at Lin, then back to Alma.

"I agreed to provide the information you require, and so I will. I do not have that information on hand, but it can be easily attained once we return to my home world."

I glared at her, but she just smiled at me. There was nothing I could do about it, and she knew so. I could refuse to fix her ship and let them all die, or I could fix it and hope she gave me the information. Either way I wouldn't get what I wanted ... at least not right now.

"You did not deal straight with me, and you know it," I said. "I will fix your ship and escort you home, but I want that information, no more tricks."

Alma smiled and nodded. "Of course. I will provide the information you require the moment we are home. Thank you for your patience."

"And Lin comes back to my ship with me."

Alma nodded again. "As you wish."

I didn't think she cared much either way, but I would need Lin to corroborate my story when we contacted Lillora command. I just hoped his relationship with his father was not as bad as I imagined it might be. If it was, convincing them that any of this is not his fault may be next to impossible.

"Um, Ben," Buttercup said over our internal connection.

"Yes, what? We're a little busy here."

"Incoming."

It was all she said before there was a bend in space, then a bright white pop and Bubbles was there. I reached out and caught her midair. She gurgled in glee as soon as she laid eyes on me. Could things possibly get any more complicated?

"Thanks for the heads up. I have her."

If this continued, I would have to start bringing Bubbles with me or carry a catcher's mitt everywhere I went.

"Lin and I will see to your repairs with the Parvis. As soon as they're done, we'll return to our ship and accompany you home."

In truth, considering how this deal was going and how the rest of the crew were acting, I just wanted to be sure our new friends were safe. As soon as the Parvis were done, we would get back to Buttercup and make our call. Then, hopefully this whole mess would be behind us, and we could be on our way to the place where Bubbles could be reunited with her mother again.

THIRTY-ONE

"How did the Parvis learn so many skills?" I sat on the floor of the Peeri engine room unable to assist in the repairs. I had no knowledge of aeronautical engineering, much less alien spacecrafts, so I chatted with them instead. Once Lin guided me to the work area there wasn't much else for him to do, so he headed back to Buttercup while I hung around. I didn't feel comfortable leaving the Parvis without an escort, even if it was only a single human, a baby Viraquin and a Chitterwall who seemed to be more help than I was when it came to fetching and retrieving tools and equipment.

"It is really a part of our culture. Everyone learns a bit of everything so we can help each other, but we each grow up in clans that specialize in particular areas. Frig grew up in a medical clan, Moll grew up in an engineering clan and I grew up learning about the Nexus."

"Wait." I peered at her as she stood on a control panel. She held a miniature tablet in her hands and hair-thin wires hung out of her backpack leading to tiny electrodes on her head. "Is that what you're doing now? Connecting to the Nexus?"

"Twitch." Heshel called out from across the room. "Bring me the filament fuser from the tool bag on the floor."

I looked across the room and couldn't see any of the other Parvis working. They had all used their diminutive size to their advantage, disappearing in and among the pipes, conduit and wiring that crisscrossed and bridged in a labyrinth across the space. Everything the Peeri made seemed to have the same iridescent coloring and the parts in the engine room were no exception. Yellows, greens, purples and blues streaked every surface like pearls, lending grace and beauty to every object.

Twitch popped out from behind a thick, gray, opalescent section of pipe and scurried over to a tool bag. Without any hesitation he snatched a small tool that reminded me of a crafting glue gun, then ran back in again. I had no idea how the Chitterwall understood what he did, but there was no doubt he was probably the smartest creature on our ship next to Buttercup.

"This is a Nexus amplifier." Dash went on, oblivious to the intricacies of Twitch and his tool fetching abilities. "It allows me to see and connect on a higher level with computer systems like this one. It's very handy when I need to do a systems analysis or check for programming errors."

"Wow." I nodded in wonder. "You five are truly incredible. I will never underestimate anyone because of their size again."

"Sure you will." Dash laughed. "Everyone does. If you're big, you must be strong. If you're little, you must be weak. Look." She pointed to me sitting on the ground. "You're only here now because you assume we can't defend ourselves."

I opened my mouth to refute her claim but couldn't.

"True enough." I pulled Bubbles off my lap and went to stand. "I didn't even realize I was—"

Dash laughed again.

"You don't have to leave. I was just making an observation. It's nice to have someone different to talk to for once. Not that I don't love my friends over there, but when you are stuck in a box together you tend to get on each other's nerves."

Now it was my turn to laugh.

"You all have such a positive outlook on things considering ... well you know." I had already put my foot in my mouth enough, I didn't want to shove it in there any further by saying the wrong thing again.

"Considering we are slaves?"

"You aren't slaves anymore." I was quick to amend. "You are all free to do whatever you want from now on."

Dash smiled and worked her fingers across her tablet again. "Life is meant to be lived no matter what situation you're in. Crazy as it may seem, there is some wisdom in Captain Alma's actions. If she and her crew were going to die, why spend your last few days living in fear and misery? Enjoy life while you have it, for you never know when it might be gone."

I sat on the floor and let Bubbles get comfortable on my lap again. She looked up at me, then at Dash, swaying back and forth as she blew bubbles and danced light across her skin.

"I suppose you're right, but I can't see taking it quite as far as she did. It was like she didn't care at all. I understand living your life, but partying instead of trying to fix your ship seems a little extreme."

"Perhaps so." Dash nodded. "Why did Prince Lin refuse to join in the revelry? It seems everyone on the ship, including the captain, took part in this joy she describes. Why didn't he?"

"Lin said the secret to happiness doesn't work on him for some reason." As I said it, I felt myself feeling a little sorry for him despite where I saw everything going with the crew. "I guess it had some limited effect at first then petered out. Now he's just like us. A bunch of joyless mechanics working in the back room."

Dash laughed again. "Speak for yourself. I don't need any secret of the universe to find joy. I have it already."

"And what is it?"

She stopped typing on her tablet and pointed down to Bubbles sitting on my lap.

"Family. You have it all around you. Bubbles, Twitch, Lois, even Prince Lin. You're all family."

I smiled at her. "As far as I am concerned, you're all part of the family too."

Dash pumped her fist in the air and hopped on her toes. "You can be a part of ours too," she said. "But you're really going to have to learn to do something. No self-respecting Parvis sits on the floor when there's work to be done."

"Ouch." I snorted out a laugh.

"Family is honest." She shrugged and went back to typing on her tablet. "You're tall, maybe you can learn to change light bulbs or something."

"I know how to change a ..."

I caught her grin and knew I'd been had.

"Okay. Chalk one up for the Parvis." I smiled. "Just hurry up. I want to get out of here before another raves breaks out in the supply dock."

THIRTY-TWO

Lois met us at the airlock as Lin and I reboarded
Buttercup with our Parvis entourage. "I am so sorry.
There was nothing I could do. As soon as she woke up and
looked around, she started sparkling, then pop, she was gone."

"It's alright." I handed Bubbles to Lois and saw the bio
luminescent light slow and her face got all pinched and angry.

"Easy." I held up a hand. "I'm not going anywhere. We just
need to do a few things. Aunty Lois will take good care of you."

Lin raised one of his eyebrows which I was beginning to
take as a substitute for a smile. "She has formed quite an attach-
ment to you. It could prove to be an issue in the future. Especially if she refuses to ever be separated."

I nodded. "I have already thought of that. It's not like I can
leave her with a sitter. We'll work it out, though. For now, we
have more important things to do."

I walked toward the bridge, motioning the crew out of the
cargo hold. I smiled to myself at the thought. We really *were*
becoming a crew.

Lois moved next to me keeping pace as I walked. "What

happened on the other ship? I got worried when you didn't say anything."

"It pretty much looks like a frat house during rush week. We only saw three crew members, including the captain, and they could barely stand on their own two feet. I'm having some serious second thoughts about sending them home with this happy juice, or whatever it is."

"Unfortunately, if you choose not to escort them back, you will not be able to attain the knowledge you bargained for." Lin spoke up from behind us. "Everything you went through would have been for nothing."

I walked through the bulkhead to the bridge. "I know. I guess it'll be worth it if we find this little girl's mother." I glanced over the infant in Lois's arms. "Besides, it's not like we won't warn them first. Speaking of ..."

I turned my attention to the viewscreen where Buttercup's visual voice wave was back to its usual location.

"Can you reach out and contact the Lillora high command? Tell them we need to speak to King ..."

I looked at Lin who had taken a position next to Lois by her chair. Frig, Heshel, Molly, Dash and Jib had all climbed into the seat and were making themselves comfortable.

"King Janus Namid Izar."

I blinked. "What he said. And back us off Alma's ship. Bring us around behind her where we can keep an eye on things. I didn't get the feeling she was aggressive, but something tells me that crew is ..." I wasn't really sure what to say.

"Unpredictable." Lin finished for me, echoing the statement he made when we first met.

I was again stunned by the realization that Lin had been right all along. Not because Lin was unreliable or deceitful, but because I had been too stubborn to listen. I had to find out for myself. Had to learn the hard way and that put all of us in jeopardy.

"Unpredictable." I nodded in agreement.

The viewscreen shifted as Buttercup altered our position in relation to Alma's ship.

"We should be ready to get underway in a few minutes," I said. "I just want to be sure Lillora knows what's coming before—"

Molly let out a little scream cutting me off and I looked down to see her pointing at the view screen. When her comrades followed her gaze, the rest of the Parvis let out screams and shouts of terror as well.

I jerked my head around to see what they were looking at, expecting to see some horrible anomaly or maybe the Scavid who had won their battle and tracked us all the way here.

Instead, I saw—well, nothing. Nothing new, anyway. Only Alma's ship and the cube that had been previously obscured due to our angle of approach earlier. Now it was visible off Alma's port side where it was moored to their ship, ready to be towed to Lillora.

"That is the secret they found?" Dash grabbed hold of her blue ponytail and began stroking it with her hands.

"Yeah." I narrowed my eyes at them, still not comprehending the reason for their alarm and panic. "That's it. Why? Have you seen it before?"

Frig stepped forward, his face looking as red and furious as his jacket.

"That is no fountain of youth, nor is it the secret to happiness. It is a prison designed to hold the most dangerous creatures my people have ever encountered."

Lois, Lin and I all stared at the cube for several seconds, then I looked back to the group of terrified looking Parvis.

"Come again?"

"Humans really are slow, aren't they?" Molly, the purple Parvis stomped forward, clenching her tiny fists at her sides. "Not all intelligent life is the size of a big, gangly Earth dweller. We are all different sizes. Look at us. We are a fraction of your size. The Quix, imprisoned on that cube, are even smaller. Microscopic by comparison. We can't even see them with the naked eye. That cube was built to hold billions of the Quix, pretty much their entire civilization."

"How do you know all of this?" Lois stared at the screen with a mix of fear and wonder.

"Because we put them there," Jib said, taking up the conversation. "The Quix were banished into deep space as an ultimate punishment for their crimes against all life. There was a transponder broadcasting a warning to anyone who might wander within range, but it must have malfunctioned. That or the Quix found a way to deactivate it."

"What sort of crimes were the Quix accused of committing?" Lin stepped forward almost pushing Lois to the side. "What are they doing to Captain Amalthea and her crew?"

The thought hadn't even occurred to me. Maybe the Quix were doing something to Alma and her crew. That's why they were acting so strange.

"I wondered why there weren't any engineers present while we worked on their propulsion systems," Frig said. "Usually, an engineering crew is pretty touchy about outsiders getting into their more sensitive systems. The Quix are an invasive and intelligent race who use the Nexus to overtake a host's endocrine system, among other things. All creatures have the capacity to produce a chemical or hormone that elicits feelings of happiness or euphoria ... some more than others." He glanced at Lin with an accusing eye. "The Quix learned how to stow away on a living organism then hijack this system and kick it into overdrive."

"So, they hitch a ride and get everyone high?" I grinned, feeling somewhat vindicated about my first assessment of Alma and her crew.

"I don't understand why that's such a crime." Lois furrowed her brow as she took all of this in. "I get that they're hijacking lifeforms against their will ... which now that I say it out loud does sound pretty bad, but I'm still not sure that warrants banishing an entire civilization into deep space for all eternity."

"The Quix do not just stow away and hijack the feel-good centers of a species brain," Heshel said. "That's only a distraction to keep the host from realizing what's really happening."

"And what is that? What do they want?" Lin asked.

"Food," Molly said. "They eat their host from the inside out. They have a taste for intelligent life forms, and they prefer to dine while their food is still breathing."

Lois gasped. "It's like the Dolichogenidea xenomorph."

"The what?" I said.

"It's a wasp that injects eggs into a caterpillar. The larvae slowly eats the caterpillar from the inside out. Fascinating lifecycle."

"If you're Freddy Krueger." I winced. "That's disgusting."

"I am not familiar with the Krueger entity, but that is precisely what the Quix do." Molly continued. "They were banished because they would infest whole planets, consume an entire species and then move on to the next one. Imagine if a common disease became self-aware and as intelligent as we are. It could adapt and overcome obstacles. It would wipe out millions, all in the pursuit of its own propagation and reproduction. That is the Quix. An aggressive, selfish, homicidal, virus bent on consuming everything it can find."

"Sounds a lot like humans." I chided under my breath.

"What are we going to do?" Lois scowled at me then stared at the cube on the screen. "We have to stop them."

"Agreed." I ran a hand through my hair as I did my best to think. "These Quix are too dangerous to bring to your planet, even if we warn them. I hate to say it Lin, but you were right all along."

Lin did not smile or gloat. He just looked to the screen with Lois and glared at the unseen attackers. "Unfortunately, we have restored Alma's propulsion systems. She can be underway in a matter of minutes.

I held up a finger, putting the problem on hold for one more moment. "There is something I don't understand. Why aren't any of us affected? We were all over there, but none of us are acting like lunatics. Why didn't any of them become stowaways inside of us?"

"The Nexus." Dash answered. "If you can't access the Nexus, they can't hijack your body's internal systems. They are only able to survive inside of a host for a few seconds without this control. They subsist on the chemicals released as a result of this interaction and without them they die."

"Like holding your breath underwater," I said.

"Exactly." They can survive in an outside environment in a sort of slow hibernation state for long periods, but inside the body they have a finite time to access the chemicals they need to survive and reproduce. Lois, Twitch and, with apologies, Lin, none of you have the ability to access the Nexus so they are not a threat to you."

"And what about me?" I jerked a thumb toward my chest. "Why wasn't I infected?"

"I believe I can answer that," Buttercup injected for the first time. I forgot she had been listening to the whole conversation. Usually, she had something to say about ... well, pretty much everything, but this time she had remained studiously quiet.

"You were, in fact, infected. This would account for our communications and Nexus interruption when you first visited their ship. Not to mention your odd behavior." I thought about the loopy feeling I had when I first arrived and realized Buttercup was probably right.

"Most computer systems are not an actual intelligence, and thus would not have reasoned out a practical solution. I was able to isolate the problem and block the interference, but what I was likely doing was interfering with the Quix's ability to hijack your internal systems."

"You installed a virus scanner," I said. "And booted them out of my brain?"

"A bit prehistoric, but close enough," Buttercup said.

"What about you?" I looked to the Parvis again. "Why aren't you affected? Wait, what about Bubbles?" We all turned to stare at the glowing infant gurgling in Lois' arms.

"We are unpalatable to the Quix and I would surmise, because of her gelatinous makeup, Bubbles is as well. It was our insusceptibility that allowed us to fight and to banish the Quix in the first place."

"Well, they aren't gone yet." I gathered myself and turned to head to the cargo hold.

"Buttercup, get us over there. We need to disable their ship again so they can't go anywhere. Then we'll contact Lillora to let the Peeri know what's going on."

Before I could take three steps toward the cargo hold, the interior lights flickered, and I could hear systems begin to wind down all over the ship.

"Buttercup, what's going on? Are you okay?"

"Negative." Buttercup's voice sounded panicked and somewhat digitized, like talking on a cellphone when the connection wasn't quite there. Propulsion and Warpstream are down. Communications offline. Working to maintain life support."

Shooting pain lanced through my skull and my own vision blurred as the bridge seemed to wobble under my feet. "What? Why?" I staggered toward the screen staring out into space looking for the source of our problems, then the screen went black as well.

Something keyed in my memory about the Nexus connection Buttercup and I shared; a symbiotic link that combined her computing power with my biological intellect. Usually I wasn't even aware of the connection, but Buttercup was in real trouble, and now I felt the impact as well.

"It's the Quix." Frig looked all around, as if he could see them floating in the air. "They're here on your ship. They can't infect us, but they can still sabotage and interrupt your onboard systems. They've probably been working on them for days in case we got wise to their presence."

"Great!" I turned around, raising a hand to my head as I glanced at Lois and Lin, then to the Parvis on Lois's chair again. "What do we do?"

"Not much we can do," Frig said. "They're everywhere, and it's almost impossible to stop them."

THIRTY-THREE

"What's wrong with you?" Lois set Bubbles on my chair then hurried over to me and put her hand on my shoulder. "What's going on?"

"It's my connection with Buttercup. Right now, it feels like I have an iron spike in my head." I breathed through the pain. "Buttercup's in trouble. We have to figure out a way to help her!" I turned away from Lois and paced back and forth, squeezing my head between my palms. I found it hard to think straight, much less come up with any kind of plan. "We can't just sit here and wait for these things to kill us. How did they even know what to do?"

"They are as intelligent as you and I," Molly said. "Maybe more so, since we never considered the possibility that they have been here the whole time listening to every word we said. They knew every step of our plan. This contingency was probably on standby from the moment they realized they couldn't infect everyone on this ship."

"That's great." I resisted the urge to scratch my skin, thinking about the thousands of little green men lurking and crawling all over every surface in sight. "They couldn't stow away inside of us, so they decided to hide inside the ship instead. So, what do we do now? They're tiny. We can't shoot them, much as I would like to. What about gas?"

"I can flood … ship's compartments with carbon monoxide," Buttercup still sounded digitized, but she was there, as was my headache, but at least it wasn't getting any worse.

There was a loud buzz then, "… can produce an array of toxins … exhaust gasses from my engines."

"I hate to rain on the poison gas parade, but we would all die along with the Quix." Lois walked over and gripped the back of her chair with both hands in frustration. "And anyplace we could hide would be plenty of space for about a million of them to hide too."

The backlit walls and ceilings began to dim, and another lance of pain shot through my head.

"Can we eject them somehow?" I shouted though gritted teeth. "What about fire? We could burn the little suckers like popcorn."

"Unless you're fireproof," Molly said, "that holds the same problem as poisonous gas."

"Sorry." I squeezed my head harder. "Horrible visual, and a ridiculous idea. Just throwing things out there."

"Actually, you may be on to something." Lin held up a finger. "What about temperature fluctuations? They are small. Perhaps a frigid drop in atmospheric conditions would impact them."

Heshel stepped forward. "That might work. They are resilient, but I don't think they could cope with sustained subzero temperatures."

"Subzero?" Lois said. "Hold on. That might not work out so well for us either."

"What do you think Buttercup?" I grimaced toward the screen even though it was dark. "Can you do it?"

There was a loud buzz from the speakers making everyone wince, then a very non-Buttercup voice came over the ship's intercom.

"Surrender." The word ground out as if verbal communication were painful. "Or we will terminate the child."

My eyes shot to Bubbles. She sat in my chair with Twitch looking back at me. Her eyes went from joy to worry in the span of a second as she no doubt read the pain and horror on my face.

"Can they do that?"

When no one answered, I looked to the Parvis.

"Someone answer me! Can they kill Bubbles?"

None of them would meet my eyes.

"So that's it then. Either we kill them, or they kill all of us, Bubbles included." I solidified my resolve, feeling my lips peel away from my teeth in a snarl.

"Buttercup if you can hear me, freeze these little demons out of here right now."

My eyes went to Lois. Tears already streamed down her face. I wasn't sure if she feared for Bubbles, herself or all of us. Either way it didn't matter.

The second I gave the command, the temperature in the cabin dropped fast enough to take my breath away. Space was cold. Cold enough to freeze your tongue to the proverbial flagpole, then freeze your tongue, then freeze your face. At about five hundred below zero anything exposed to space became a perma-glacier within seconds. It took about half that time for Buttercup to exchange the ship's inner heat with the biting cold outside. Feeling the frigid temperature rush in was a grim reminder of how dangerous it really was out here. Any mishap, the smallest hull breach or loss of oxygen or drop in radiation shielding, and we were all dead. That didn't even take into account an entire civilization of microscopic aliens actively trying to murder us.

I hurried over and grabbed Bubbles and Twitch cradling them both to my body. They were not as small as the Quix, but they were small. They would succumb to the rapid temperature drop faster than we would. Pain continued to pound through my head, but I was surprised to find the cold actually helped a little in that regard. The torment had receded from a ten to an eight and a half.

Lois and Lin seemed to have the same idea and crouched onto the floor so the Parvis could take shelter with them.

I hurried to join them, already shivering so hard I could hardly keep my teeth from chattering. I pulled Bubbles and Twitch closer, and we all squeezed together as much as we could.

"What if Buttercup is too far gone to bring us back?" Lois said. "She's going to have to sustain this temperature for long enough to kill the Quix. We might not make it."

I couldn't believe how cold it had gotten in such a short time. Twitch was all but crawling into my shirt, but Bubbles didn't even seem bothered. Then it dawned on me. Of all of us here, she was the most adapt to survive something like this. The Viraquin were built to travel through space. This was nothing more than a summer vacation for her.

I let out a laugh and Lois glanced over at me. Her face was twisted with confusion, but she no longer shivered. Come to think of it neither did I. Ice formed around my mouth but somehow it felt marginally warmer. Was Buttercup bringing the temperature back up already. It seemed too soon, but she would know best. I tried to tell the woman sitting next to me it would be alright, but I couldn't remember her name. And the tall man sitting next to her. Why was he here? This strange fellow looked worse than all of us. He had his chin buried in his chest, and he seemed to be sleeping, though I could not imagine sleeping at a time like this ... could I? I was so tired. Maybe if I closed my eyes for a little while ... what was the ship's name? It was definitely getting warmer, so why was I so sleepy? I'd just rest for a minute, then we could all get up and go aga ...

THIRTY-FOUR

My eyes fluttered open, and I found myself staring at a slick blue ceiling. The world came back to me slowly: light, voices somewhere far away, warmth, lots of warmth, tiny hands slapping me in the face, something jumping on my chest.

I struggled to raise my head and saw Twitch hopping up and down as if my sternum were a trampoline. "What are you doing? Where is ..."

Then it hit me. Lois, Lin, Bubbles and all the others. The Quix and Buttercup freezing them out in the cold. My brain struggled to reboot, but my headache was gone. My joints protested to any sort of movement but I forced my head to the side so I could look around.

Lin stirred to my left and next to him laid Lois. She was on her back, surrounded by the Parvis who seemed frantic in their efforts to wake her up.

"Ben!" A tiny voice shrieked in my ear, making me wince. It was Dash, the Blue Parvis. She slapped my face, trying to get my attention. "Wake up. Lois is in trouble. She needs your help."

That was enough to jolt me upright. I sat up suddenly comprehending the scene. Lin was waking up on his own, but Lois wasn't. She wasn't moving at all.

My joints screamed in agony and all but refused to function, but I rolled over and managed to crawl to her, then nudged the other Parvis out of my way. "Let me see."

I pressed my fingers to her neck. She had a pulse. It was weak but it was there. Her chest wasn't moving, however. Lois wasn't breathing.

"Lois?"

I bent over her, pinched her nose and blew in two quick breaths, watching her chest rise and fall. "Come on Lois. Please don't do this. Don't die. I need you here."

I blew in two more breaths.

"I should have thought this out more." My voice squeaked with panic and tears. "I should have never let Buttercup freeze the cabin. I wasn't thinking straight. I'm so sorry."

Two more breaths. Lin was up now and watching me. So were the Parvis. There was nothing they could do. Lois was going to die, and I had caused it.

"Please Lois!" I screamed this time, not caring how it came out. The plea sounded shocking and desperate ... more desperate than I'd ever been in my life.

Two more breaths, but this time she coughed when I sat up. Weak at first, then she choked and turned to her side.

"Lois!" I threw my arms around her. Tears ran down my face as she gasped in huge breaths of air, filling her lungs with life. "Lois, I'm so glad you're all right."

"What happened?" She struggled to turn over and sit up, but I held a gentle hand to her shoulder.

"You should rest," I said. "You weren't breathing. I had to give you mouth to mouth. How do you feel?"

Frig and the other Parvis rushed in on the other side of Lois, taking her pulse and monitoring her vital signs with some sort of miniature equipment.

"I think she's going to be okay." Frig said, then hurried around to retrieve something else from his pack.

"Considering I was dead, I don't feel too bad." Lois grinned up at me. Twitch scurried over and stood on her chest, chittering his delight at seeing her conscious. Something bumped the side of my leg, and I looked over to see Bubbles had skittered across the floor to join us, too. She seemed no worse for wear. Her eyes were as bright as her smile and the bioluminescent light danced and flashed across her skin in happy little waves.

"I am fine as well." Lin sat next to Lois. "Thank you for asking."

I let out a laugh and wiped my eyes. "I'm glad you're okay. I'm glad everyone is all ri—" Then I remembered the last member of our crew, and maybe the most important.

"Buttercup!" I turned my head so I could peek at the display screen between the chairs. "Are you there? Are you all right?"

"I am here. Systems are marginal."

I got to my knees so I could see the screen a little more clearly.

"What do you mean by marginal? Did it work? Did we get rid of those rotten little stowaways?"

"Once I was aware of the Quix, I was able to alter my internal monitoring systems to detect the microscopic entity. As of now, I am not detecting any Quix onboard the ship either in the cabin or among my internal systems. I believe we have destroyed them."

Lois sat up, resting her weight back on her hands. "How

many were there? I mean they were an intelligent species. How many of the Quix did we kill?"

"It is impossible to attain an accurate count due to their size, however I estimate there were more than twenty million infesting the ship."

Lois let out a breath. "What?" We just killed twenty million intelligent creatures? That's like killing every living human in New York."

She put her face in her hands and started to cry. I laid a hand on her back, doing my best to comfort her, but I did not feel the remorse that she did.

"Listen, it doesn't matter whether there were twenty or twenty million of them. They were trying to kill us. They were all working together to take our lives. You, me, Bubbles, Lin, the Parvis. We would all be dead right now if we hadn't defended ourselves."

"I was almost dead too," Lois snapped. "Don't forget that."

I closed my eyes and sighed. I could never forget that.

"I'm sorry I took such a drastic action, but I didn't know what else to do."

"You can think things through," Lois said. "Consider the repercussions of your actions. Stop putting us all in danger without an intelligent, rational plan. You're going to get us all killed if you keep doing this."

I looked at her and nodded. "You're right. I'm sorry. I'll try to do better."

"Forgive me," Buttercup interrupted. "But I am afraid there is still a matter that requires your immediate attention."

I glanced toward the screen, remembering Alma and her ship full of Quix.

"Right. Let's contact Lillora high command and tell them what's happening. Maybe they will have some—"

"Negative." Buttercup interrupted. "Communication and shields are both down. The Quix managed catastrophic damage to many of my systems. I am currently focusing power and resources to repairing life support, computer systems and propulsion."

"Okay, can we at least get a message to Alma somehow and let her know—"

"Negative." Buttercup interrupted again. "Captain Amalthea is underway to Lillora. She is out of range and moving under full power."

"What?" I shot to my feet as Buttercup brought up a display of empty space where Alma's ship had been.

Lin rose to his feet as well, pulsing his wings in nervous vibrations. "We cannot allow that ship to reach Lillora. My people will be annihilated."

I turned to the screen again. "Can we catch them? Is our Warpstream drive online?"

"Affirmative."

Finally, some good news.

"The Peeri ship is also capable of Warpstream travel, however, and they have a substantial head start thanks to the Quix's sabotage of my systems. According to my calculations, the trip to Lillora will take approximately ninety-one hours. We will not arrive before Captain Amalthea."

I backhanded my chair in frustration.

Lois stood up next to me, grabbing my other arm for support. Her words rang in my ears. I didn't want to be impulsive, but at this point I didn't know what else to do.

"We have to try. Power up the Warpstream and get us to Lillora as fast as you can. At least we can get underway, then discuss what to do when we get there."

THIRTY-FIVE

"How close are we?" I sat in my chair, with Lois and Lin in their chairs to my right and left respectively. Bubbles sat with me while the Parvis were split between Lois and Lin, riding on their laps, everyone watching the screen with as much expectation as I was. If we kept picking up new passengers at this rate, I would have to start setting up lawn chairs for everyone to sit in.

"Forty minutes out," Buttercup said. "Alma's ship has already arrived, though without our communications array I cannot tell if they have made contact."

"Can't we get there any faster?" I urged, sliding to the edge of my seat.

"Normally I would drop out of the Warpstream outside of the Peeri solar system in order to prevent a collision with unrecorded debris fields or ships passing through the area. Dropping out next to Lillora would be much faster, but we risk a catastrophic incident."

"How much will it cut our time?"

"We would arrive in three minutes. However, our shield

systems are still down. It is unlikely we would survive any impact."

Lois' earlier words hung heavy on my shoulders. I had just promised to take things easier. To be smart and stop taking chances and here we were, ready to throw the dice again. I looked to her for an answer, but she stared back at me with wide, unanswering eyes. Much as I wanted to honor her and keep everyone safe, I had little choice if we were going to have any chance to save Lin's entire civilization. "Do it, Buttercup. If we don't get there before the Peeri board that ship, the Quix could destroy their entire planet."

"Acknowledged."

"I don't mean to be indelicate," Frig said from Lois's lap. "But everyone on that ship is likely dead. The Quix can extend the length of time it takes to consume a host, but they cannot stop it. It's a miracle anyone on that ship lasted as long as they did."

"The navigation system on that ship is programmable." Lin looked on as we forged ahead through the Warpstream. "Once Captain Amalthea set her course, nothing else would be required. The ship would travel to its destination and stop to await further orders, or in this case, a union with the Peeri command ship."

"And how many Quix are stowed away on that ship?" Lois asked. "I mean now that they have had time to ..." She paused and swallowed hard. "Eat and breed."

"According to my calculations," Buttercup answered. "There could be trillions of Quix prepared to launch an invasion on Lillora."

I knew what Lois was thinking. If we were forced to destroy that ship, how many Quix would we be killing. How could we wipe out an entire race of intelligent beings? I was thinking the same thing, but this was war, even if Lillora didn't know it yet. If we didn't prevent the Quix from reaching the Peeri, they might be unstoppable. Not just here, but throughout the universe.

"Dropping out of Warpstream," Buttercup announced. "Prepare for impact."

I held my breath as the automated seatbelt system rolled over my lap and shoulders. It did nothing to restrain Bubbles so I held her tight, thinking it would be better than nothing given the fact that our entire ship would disintegrate if we hit anything larger than a pebble. Even then ...

The colorful aurora lights playing across the screen dissipated over the hull and the Peeri solar system came into view. Planets, asteroids, moons and satellites streaked by way too fast to be avoided if any were in our path. As Buttercup altered her speed and trajectory Lillora came into view as well.

I let out my breath in a woosh, grateful we had not been reduced to a flaming comet and took in the scene before us. Lillora was a beautiful ball of blues, violets and whites streaked with gorgeous bodies of water and land. I would have taken more time to admire it, but for the activity playing out in front of it.

An entire armada of Peeri ships had turned out to greet the incoming exploration vessel. They formed a half circle around Alma's ship, almost as if they were prepared to fire, but I could tell this wasn't the case. There was another ship. A bulky troop carrier, covered in flags and decorations, no doubt designed to transport delegates to greet new and important arrivals. It may even have the king himself onboard.

"Do we have comms yet?" I shouted, seeing that the delegate ship would dock in a matter of moments.

"Negative." Buttercup sounded every bit as frantic as I felt.

"We have no way of communicating with the Peeri high command."

I looked at Lois again. "What do I do?"

She shrugged her shoulders and worked her jaw opened and closed but nothing came out.

"This is crazy. We did all of this to keep Bubbles safe and get her to her mother but all I've done is put her at risk ... put us all at risk. If we charge in, everyone on this ship could die. If we turn away, The Quix will destroy Lin's entire planet. It's an impossible decision." I dropped my face into my hands. "We're supposed to be keeping a low profile. Why can't we just take Bubbles home without blundering through half the aliens in the universe?"

No one said anything for a moment, then much to my surprise it was Lin who spoke up, breaking the silence with a smooth calming voice.

"You have done a great deal for me, and the Peeri people."

I turned to look at him. He had risen from his chair, leaving Jib, Dash and Molly remaining to stand in his seat.

"I would not endeavor to ask more, but I will offer this advice as it pertains to your earlier discussion about taking risks."

He tore his gaze from the screen and looked at me, tears welling in his eyes as his wings rose to their natural position, giving him a regal, yet vulnerable appearance as he spoke.

"You are on a quest for the impossible. You seek not glory, but a righteous goal, and to reach it, you will encounter innumerable challenges. Shrink from any one of them and you will fail. Fear disaster and you will invite it to your door. A quest such as yours cannot be accomplished without the aid of others, and with that comes responsibility. To gain support and trust you must earn it. You can only do that by risking yourselves. I ask not that you do me this favor, but that you do what is right. Save my people and fear not the consequences, but rather look to your victory, and see through your quest to find this child's home."

I stared at him for a moment, then released my restraints and stood with him. I held Bubbles in my arm and turned to Lois. Her expression had changed from fear to resolve. She did not stand, but instead pulled up her weapons array screens and gave me a single nod.

I turned to the forward display and watched the delegate ship as it approached Alma's ship.

"Shield status report?"

"Shields and communications are both down." Buttercup's voice was cold and resolute. "All weapons are operational."

"Target Alma's ship. Hit it with everything we have and don't leave anything to chance. Just make sure you don't hit that delegate vessel. If we're going to make it out of this thing alive, we can't so much as snag a single flag, or that row of Peeri warships will obliterate us before we can so much as wave goodbye."

THIRTY-SIX

The merciless volley of fire we unleashed on Alma's defenseless ship was horrifying to watch. Even though she and her crew had been consumed by the Quix, seeing the ship suffer such an unprovoked attack was sickening. Green energy bolts tore through her hull while a single Skipper missile streaked toward its target. None of the Peeri had a chance to defend her. The solitary seismic charge ripped the ship to pieces, sending huge chunks of shrapnel spiraling into space. No one could have survived such an attack, not even the Quix.

The prison cube was sent tumbling away, detached but intact as Alma's ship disintegrated from the blast. I opened my mouth to have Lois reacquire the new target, but Buttercup interrupted me.

"We have multiple missile locks. Taking evasive action."

"No, wait." I held out a hand. "Can the Peeri ships detect our weapons systems?"

I looked at Lin still standing to my left.

He nodded once.

"Power down all weapons. We don't have any shields so I assume they can see that too. We can't talk to them, so our best bet is to appear as nonthreatening as possible."

"I'm not sure how nonthreatening we can be when we just destroyed one of their ships." Lois dropped her hands from the virtual displays and they disappeared from view as our weapons systems went offline.

I stared at the row of huge Peeri crafts. "There must be a dozen or more warships out there, not including the delegate ship. We are fish in a barrel. It's a miracle we aren't dead already."

"Peeri vessels are holding position," Buttercup said. "What would you have me do now?"

"Just don't move. Don't even sneeze. I have a feeling even a wing twitch will bring down enough laser fire to jumpstart the big bang."

"We can't just sit here." Lois sat forward in her seat and turned toward me. Frig and Heshel jumped off her lap then ran to join Jib, Molly and Dash on Lin's chair.

"I concur." Buttercup's sine wave vibrated on the viewscreen in front of us. "Sooner or later, someone is going to flinch and there is almost no scenario in which we will come out in one piece."

"Any progress on those comms? It would be great to get a little face time with that delegation ship."

"Negative. The Quix were thorough in damaging the communications array. I have not been able to repair it."

"I'm sure our radio silence is not helping matters." Lois stood and stared at the armada of formidable Peeri ships. "They're probably hailing us like crazy and think we're ignoring them."

"Considering what I know about you, Lin." I let out a

humorless chuckle. "I doubt that is going over all that well. No offense."

"None taken. You are correct. The Peeri will take our silence as an insult and will likely respond to our insolence with weapons fire."

"Great." I threw out my arms. "We can't fight ... not that I want to, and we can't talk to them. What are we supposed to do?"

Frig cleared his throat and I turned to look at the five Parvis. Up until now, they had remained silent, but the red leader stepped forward, placing his hands on his hips.

"We may have an idea, if you will permit us."

Lois, Lin and I all stared at them for a moment. Then I shrugged. "Well, it's not like anyone else has any ideas. Go ahead."

Heshel and Molly leapt forward, landing on the floor. They ran toward the control panel in front of my chair while the other three motioned for Lin to come back and have a seat in his usual position again.

"Give those two a boost up to your touch screen." Frig pointed to the Parvis headed toward the front of the bridge. "They will try to do something about the communications issue while we work with Lin."

"Work with Lin? How are you going to fix the comms when Buttercup can't? She literally *is* the ship."

Lois crouched and boosted Molly and Heshel up to the tabletop touchscreen and they went to work, making virtual connections to circuits through the interface.

Buttercup could sense and see everything they were doing, and I wondered if she would allow them the access they needed without a fight. Then she let out a gasp.

"Genius. I can't believe I did not think of that."

"What?" I stared at the array of lights, buttons, graphs and gauges. "What did they do? Can we talk to them now?"

Bubbles gurgled in my arm, and I turned around to set her in my chair so I could spin her out of sight, in case an angry Peeri suddenly appeared on screen.

"The delegation ship is falling back," Buttercup reported, sounding urgent. "The warships are likely preparing to fire."

"Whatever you're going to do, you better do it now," I said.

Molly began to tap at a big red button that appeared on the panel. I looked around the bridge, scrutinized the controls and stared at the screen, but for the life of me I couldn't tell what she was doing. Then I noticed a subtle difference around the edges of the forward display as she tapped. It got lighter and darker each time she hit her button.

"You're sending Morse Code." I marveled at the Parvis's engineering and creativity. "Somehow you rigged Buttercup's external lighting, and you're sending them a message."

I spun Bubbles around so she could see. "Look at this. We're talking like you do."

Bubbles seemed unimpressed as she regained her balance from the sudden spin.

"I don't know what Morse Code is," Molly said. "But yes. I am signaling to them with the lights outside the ship. I am sending them a universal sign of peace and surrender."

"Do you think they'll buy it?" Lois stared at the screen. "I mean we destroyed one of their ships. Peace and surrender seem a little ... I don't know, like we're lying just to escape, or getting ready to shoot them."

I watched as the delegation ship paused to turn toward us, as if looking at our display.

"I think it's working," I said. "If we can get them to delay their attack long enough for Buttercup to—"

"The Peeri warships are confirming missile lock and the delegate ship is continuing its retreat."

I looked up and sure enough the delegate ship began to turn away again.

"No!" I shouted. "Wait. You can't ignore a white flag. Isn't there some kind of law—"

"Any law precluding them from firing upon us was superseded by our attack on their vessel," Buttercup interrupted. "I suggest we take immediate evasive action, or we will have no hope."

"It doesn't matter." I slammed my fist on the control panel between the two Parvis, still frantically trying to signal the Peeri ships. "We can't outrun that many guns. There must be something else we can do."

Then almost as if by magic, the delegate ship made an abrupt turn and started heading in our direction.

"Warships are disengaging." Buttercup's astounded voice came over the speakers, slow and deliberate. "Missile lock no longer detected. All weapons systems are powering down."

I pulled my fist back and stared at it, then I looked at the two Parvis standing on the control panel. "What did you tell them?"

They smiled and pointed at the chair behind me. I turned to see Lin all wired up with electrodes to his head and temples. Tiny wires traced their way down to the backpack Dash always wore and she had a touchscreen control pad in her hand. It was the Nexus amplifier I had seen her use on herself, but now it was on Lin. She smiled but not at me. Her grin pointed up at Lin and he had more raw emotion on his face than I ever thought possible.

"I did it," he said. "I felt the Nexus. It was weak but I got a message through to my father. He knows I am on this ship, and he is sending the delegates to meet us."

I stared at him, my mouth agape. "I thought ..."

Rather than finish, I made a vague motion with my hand hoping that would sum up the bulk of my confusion.

Dash looked at me as Frig disconnected his medical monitoring apparatus. "Lin said he could not connect, but you mentioned something that made me wonder. You said he suffered some minor effects when they first encountered the cube. The Quix may not have been able to infect him, but he must have had some limited capabilities, or he would have never felt anything at all. The Quix would not have been able to take advantage of a severely weakened Nexus ability, but I can. My amplifier allowed Lin to make contact, at least momentarily. I feel confident they will be able to engineer a permanent solution to his issue now that we know the problem."

"Do you know what you've done?" I fell to my knees in front of Dash and bent to kiss her blue-haired head.

Dash ducked a little then laughed, straightening her hat. "You're welcome. Just don't do that anymore."

I laughed and peered at Lois. She smiled too, hugging Bubbles in celebration.

"We aren't completely out of the woods," I said. "But at least they aren't going to blast us into space junk. I'm sure with Lin's help we'll be able to explain everything and hopefully we can still find a way to get Bubbles home to her mother."

Lin looked at me. "Thank you."

He sat straight on his chair and put on his formal face though there were tears of joy in his eyes. "You and the others have given me more than you could ever know. I will do everything in my power to be sure that debt is paid. Given I am an outcast in my family, I am not sure what that will look like, but I assure you, if it is in my power, you will have it."

I nodded. "That's good enough for me."

I stood and Lois helped pull some of the tiny electrodes off his head. "Let's get you ready to meet your people. We have a lot of explaining to do, and if Ben does all the talking, we'll be right back to staring down the barrel of laser again."

THIRTY-SEVEN

Once the warships decided against turning us into a big pile of space debris, the troop transport originally destined for Alma's ship turned and headed in our direction. It was loaded with a contingent of military guards and three delegates who were prepared to greet a very ... unpredictable Peeri captain. As it turned out, it was also the perfect contingent to make first contact with us.

There were a few tense moments during our introduction, but once the delegates were on board, we spent hours explaining and re-explaining our situation. The first order of business was to convince them that under no circumstances should they approach the cube. At least not until the Parvis had a chance to explain in detail about the Quix and how they could infiltrate not only Alma's crew, but their entire civilizations.

I was full of urgent gratitude from the moment they arrived. After all, they had spared our lives and we had so much to tell them. After rehashing the same story for hours on end, I was amazed at how fast gratitude could turn to frustration. It wasn't as if they didn't understand or believe us. I just got the sense they were stalling for time. When we were invited to dock with a much larger ship that had approached under heavy guard, I understood why.

"Please do not insult my father."

I looked over at Lin as we waited for the airlock to normalize. "Why would I do that?"

"I do not believe you would do it on purpose." Lin continued, keeping his eyes forward and his wings smoothed down to his back. "I am only asking that you exercise caution when speaking to the king."

Lois let out a snicker behind us. "It didn't take long for him to figure you out."

I gasped. "I'm the one insulted here, thank you very much. Ben Roberts is more than capable of being respectful."

"Just the same, perhaps you should allow me to filter any responses." Buttercup interjected over the speaker. "Don't worry. They will not be able to intercept the transmission."

"No. I will not take political advice from the ship who always wants to shoot first and ask questions later. You all trust me, right?"

I looked at the Parvis standing next to Lois. They offered a collective shrug.

"Great. Well, I know Twitch has faith in me." I held up a hand and the little Chitterwall stood on my shoulder to give me a high-five. "Thanks buddy. Keep a close eye on Bubbles back there. If she looks like she's going to go supernova on us, let me know."

I wore the backpack Buttercup had designed and Bubbles rode inside. I knew it was dangerous to bring her along, but leaving her in the ship always resulted in a surprise appearance. At least this way she was already here. Hopefully she would remain out of sight.

The airlock opened and we stepped through. I stared in awe at the vision before me. We had all watched the ship approach on the viewscreen. It was easily ten times the size of Buttercup, maybe more. What I didn't expect was that the entire ship would be one giant compartment the size of a football stadium.

The royal envoy had been designed for one thing and one thing only. Ceremony.

We walked along a center aisle carpeted in bright yellow. Peeri lined up in groups on either side in sections, wearing colorful uniforms of red, green, purple, blue and gold. They stood in tight, perfectly ordered squares, unflinching as a huge chorus of tribal drums beat out a royal cadence. The sound echoed off of the cavernous walls like thunder drowning out any thought of a whisper between the regimented assembly.

Long ebony tapestries hung from unbelievably high ceilings and the white walls gleamed so bright I wanted to squint. If I hadn't walked through the airlock of my own ship, I would have sworn we were in a roman colosseum built for a modern-day emperor.

"Wow," I said. "Does your dad rent this place out for picnics? I bet he really impresses the chicks with this thing. It's way better than a Ferrari."

Lin groaned.

"Perhaps you should allow Lois to do all of the talking while you are here," Buttercup said at the same time.

"I'm kidding, guys, relax. Everything is going to be great. Me and the king are going to be best buds, don't worry."

"We are going to die," Frig piped up from behind us. "If they start shooting, scatter. We're small. They'll hit the big ones first."

I was about to offer another reassuring retort when Lin bumped my shoulder, regaining my attention. I looked over in time to see him lowering to one knee and bowing his head in reverence. A quick survey of my surroundings revealed a wide set of stairs leading to a large dais in front of us. Lois and the Parvis had taken a knee as well, leaving me standing all alone.

Maybe Frig was right. I probably should've hung back on this one.

I jetted to one knee so fast I fell more than bowed, requiring me to throw my hands to the floor to steady myself and stop my momentum.

Lin groaned again.

We remained on our knees for what seemed like a full minute. I wanted to look up to see what was going on. When I started to move, Lin made a curt noise under his breath. This was ridiculous. If I knelt much longer, I would fall asleep.

Finally, a voice came from just in front of us.

"You may rise."

I watched Lin out of the corner of my eye. When he rose, so did I. The bright interior made me squint, but when my eyes adjusted to the light, I saw a Peeri standing before me all clad in black like Lin, but his regalia was adorned with a cape and row after row of colorful military style medals. It reminded me of an odd mix of ancient Chinese with modern military culture.

Behind him stood a line of Peeri guards, armed with a bladed sword sheathed at their waist and a rifle held at the ready across their chests. They were garbed in the same black uniform as Lin, only they looked far more severe and menacing.

"My aids tell me I have you to thank for saving my people and restoring my son's honor."

I had to bite the inside of my cheek to keep from telling him Lin's honor was never in question.

"It was our pleasure, your Highness. I'm glad we arrived in time. I regret only that we failed to prevent the horrible tragedy caused by the Quix onboard Captain Amalthea's exploration vessel."

Who said I couldn't be diplomatic.

"The loss of Captain Amalthea Eris Thalassa was indeed a tragedy, but such is the price of knowledge."

I bit the inside of my cheek again to keep from saying something I'd regret as he shrugged away the lives of every single soul aboard that ship as if they meant nothing.

"Am I to understand you made some kind of bargain with Captain Amalthea before she died?"

I took a breath and tried to keep my face neutral. No wonder Lin was so uptight, if he had to constantly live up the expectations of a Peeri like this.

"Yes. We obtained parts and repaired her ship in exchange for information."

"And was this before or after you fired on and destroyed her vessel?"

I felt my chest tighten and the breath went out of my lungs. Were we being maneuvered into a trap? I thought we would be rewarded for saving his people, but this felt more like an inquisition.

"That would be before we fired on the ship, saving your entire planet from possible extinction."

Lin's head twitched in my direction, but I didn't break eye contact with the king.

After a moment of glaring, King Janus nodded. "As you did not fulfill your promise to deliver Captain Amalthea Eris Thalassa safely to her home port, I am disinclined to honor her agreement."

King Janus turned his back to walk away, but I took a step forward to stop him. Lin grabbed my arm just as the king's guard leveled their rifles at my head.

"Wait a minute," I demanded, ignoring the guard. "We risked out lives to help her and to save you and your people."

"I told you," Frig whispered. "Get ready to scatter."

"You're not going to walk away from us," I finished, but didn't try to move any further. "At the very least you owe my crew a little gratitude."

The king stopped, then turned to look at me. He thought for a moment, then stepped back down to where we stood. The guard took their cue and returned to a ready stance, but I knew they were prepared to defend their king if I flinched the wrong way.

"Perhaps you are right. You did save my people and I do owe you a debt of gratitude for returning my son to his station as prince of this court. Now that he can join the Nexus, he will be reunited with me here on Lillora."

Lin's grip on my arm weakened then fell. Somehow, I felt the dread in his reaction even though his father's acceptance was all he ever strived for.

"I will grant the answer to your question."

He stared at me expectantly and I looked at him, then Lois nudged my arm. "Well, what are you waiting for?"

"Oh," I said. "You mean now. Sorry. Right."

"Maybe you should all return to the ship while you are ahead." Buttercup cut in.

"It's fine." I cleared my throat and lowered my voice. "I've got this."

I leaned forward slightly. I didn't want to broadcast my question to everyone in the room if I could help it. His guard would hear and that was bad enough.

"We are looking for a Viraquin who was injured in a horrible battle. She placed her child in our care, but we don't know how or where to look for the mother in order to reunite them. Is there a place where a Viraquin might go to heal or recuperate? Do they have a home world or a place where they seek solace or peace from the outside universe?"

King Janus considered for a moment, then nodded. "There is such a place, but the location is not among even our vast knowledge, I am afraid."

I felt frustration and anger rise into my throat, but I swallowed it down as King Janus continued.

"There is, however, a people who travel the vast expanses of the universe, the lengths of which no other species has ever matched. They are obligated by their edict to work in secrecy, however considering your circumstances, they may be convinced to make an exception. I will transfer coordinates and information to your ship."

I was not happy about having to go on another wild goose chase, but at least it wasn't a dead end. If it got us closer to finding Bubbles' mother, then so be it.

"Thank you, King Janis." Another thought occurred to me, and I raised a finger eliciting a flinch from the guard.

"I do have one other question. The infant seems to have an innate ability to travel to unpredictable locations, however we are unsure why. Is there a way to focus her ability to speed up our travel and get her home?"

King Janus laughed. "To that I have a simple and direct answer."

I smiled thinking we were finally going to get something useful out of this trip after all.

"And I would be happy to provide that information in exchange for a small favor."

I threw up my hands, making the guards flinch again. "Nope. Never mind. I don't want to know. No offense but the last small favor I did for the Peeri almost got us all killed."

King Janus shrugged. "So be it. If you ever have need of such information, you know where I am."

With that, his royal pompousness turned around and split the guard as he retreated. As soon as he passed, the guard turned to follow. I watched them depart up the stairs and through a doorway at the top, then disappear. It wasn't until I turned around that I realized everyone in the room but me had bowed as he made his way out.

Oh well. I guess diplomacy wasn't really my thing.

Lois and the Parvis got to their feet and Twitch sat on my shoulder.

"You going to be okay here, Lin?" I leveled a worried eye at him. "I don't mean to offend, but your dad is a real tool. You're welcome to come with us if you want to get away."

Lin actually snorted out a laugh. "I will be fine. This is where I belong. Life will be difficult, but thanks to Dash's amplifier, I will take over for my father someday, and maybe I can make a few changes."

"Wow," Lois said. "I can say I knew Prince Lin."

"Someday you will say you know King Lintang if all goes well." He raised one eyebrow.

"I hope everything works out for you." I reached out to shake his hand and smiled, then I pulled him in for a hug. He went stiff as a board for a second, but then he relaxed and returned the sentiment.

When we parted, he had an uncomfortable smile on his face. "The court will be talking about that for quite some time."

Lois didn't miss her chance to hug him too. "Might as well give them two to talk about."

"Indeed. I will miss you all as well." Lin crouched and shook each of the Parvis's hands. "Especially you Dash. Thank you so much. If there is ever anything I can do for you ..."

Dash smiled. "I sort of like the idea of having a Peeri promise in my pocket. I will remember. And you are welcome."

"Well, I suppose this is goodbye," Lin said, as he rose to his feet. "I wish you well and say hello to Stella if you happen to see him."

The Parvis turned to make their way to the airlock, but I paused with Lois, my brow knitted in confusion. "Why would we see Stella?"

"The planet my father spoke of. It is Stella's home world. The origin of the Dazbog and what you refer to as Santa Claus."

I laughed for a second then stopped when I saw the serious look on his face as he waved goodbye. "Hold on. Are you telling me we're going to a Santa Planet?"

Lois grabbed my arm and pulled me away. "Come on. I want to get out of here. This place gives me the creeps. Let's go before they decide we would be better off staying along with Lin." The Parvis had already made their way through the procession and were in the airlock. They must have run the whole way.

I looked back and waved to Lin as the airlock door closed. I was sad to see him go but glad he had finally gotten what he wanted. I just hoped it was all he wished for.

As for us, we had our destination. Santa planet. A place and a people who might know where to find the Viraquin. Space travel was so weird.

———

Don't let your space adventure end here. See what happens when Ben and Lois learn the truth about Santa.
Yuletide Space Ranger

THANKS FOR READING!

☺ Loved the ride?
Tell the galaxy! Leaving a quick review for *Stowaway Star Runner* helps other readers discover the madness—and means the universe to this author.

Love *Stowaway Star Runner*? Don't drift away just yet! 🚀
Join the **C.G. Harris Legion** for insider access to sneak peeks of upcoming books, top-secret story intel, exclusive giveaways, and of course, Hula Harry's legendary Drink of the Week 🍸 (it's weird, wild, and probably neon).
🔗 https://www.cgharris.net/legion-sign-up-page

Craving more chaos, baby aliens, and sarcastic AI? Find out what happens next to Ben, Lois and Lois in *Yuletide Space Ranger*.

Who knew babysitting an alien would be so hard? Ben and the crew have set course for an alien planet, but the inhabitants are far from what they expected. They have answers that could get their baby Viraquin home but Ben isn't sure he's willing to pay the price for the well guarded secret.

Download the exclusive prequel novella, **Fugitive Star Voyage,** for free and discover how the madness began.

(https://dl.bookfunnel.com/fh4fi73370)

CRAVE ADVENTURE AND MAYHEM?
OPEN A C.G. HARRIS BOOK

Hell's worst government agency

Saving the galaxy was never the plan, but neither was stealing a starship.

An empire built on fear meets the one hero it never saw coming.

HULA HARRYS DEVILISH DRINKS
SINFUL SIPS FROM THE UNDERWORLD

Welcome to Hula Harry's, the only tiki bar in Hell bold enough to serve drinks that burn twice. Inside this wickedly funny cocktail book, you'll find real, mixable recipes inspired by the chaos, characters, and dark humor of The Judas Files.

These are full-throttle hellfire cocktails—The Brimstone Mary, The Dumpster Fire, and more—each crafted to ignite your taste buds and maybe your dignity. Every drink is a real-world recipe with an infernal twist, perfect for fans who like their cocktails strong and their fiction delightfully twisted.

So pull up a barstool, ignore the smoke seeping from the floorboards, and let Hula Harry mix you something unforgettable. Because in Hell's favorite bar, the drinks are real, the laughs are loud, and the hangovers are legendary.

THE C.G. HARRIS LEGION — RECRUITMENT BRIEFING

You made it to the end of the book.
You survived the chaos.
You're exactly the kind of reader we want in the **C.G. Harris Legion**.

Thousands have already joined this elite squad of readers....
now it's your turn.

WHAT YOU GET AS A LEGION RECRUIT

Exclusive intel — early chapters, secret files, bonus stories

Giveaways & prizes — only for Legion members

Hula Harry's Drink of the Week — dangerously delicious

First alerts on new releases, Kickstarters, and launches

No cost. No spam. Just fun, chaos, and insider access.

Proceed to the next page for further instructions.

TO ACCEPT YOUR MISSION:

Scan the code.
Join the chaos.

ABOUT C.G. HARRIS
CHUCK HARRELSON & KERRIE FLANAGAN

Hold onto your warp drives and wizard hats. Chuck Harrelson and Kerrie Flanagan are the award-winning coauthor team of C.G. Harris, responsible for some of the most thrilling escapades in the multiverse! Together they take readers on a devilishly daring dive into the hellish world of *THE JUDAS FILES*, a wild ride through young adult dystopia with *THE RAX*, and a space pirate adventure full of cosmic swashbuckling action in *THE VIRAQUIN VOYAGE*.

When they're not busy crafting the next great American novel or penning a haiku about the existential dread of Mondays, you can find them in the throes of what could only be described as a culinary Cold War, fiercely debating which is the superior pie—New York's big, floppy, fold-it-like-a-news-paper slice or Chicago's deep-dish cheese casserole with a crust.

To this day the debate remains unresolved. But in the heated exchange of doughy discourse, one thing becomes clear: when it comes to pizza, the only real winner is whoever gets the last slice.

Got a burning question? A wild theory? A brilliant plot twist we *absolutely* need to write? Reach out—we'd love to hear from you: **CGharrisAuthor@gmail.com**

Want in on exclusive stories, sneak peeks at upcoming chaos, and book deals that'll make your TBR list cry for mercy?

www.ingramcontent.com/pod-product-compliance
Lightning Source LLC
Chambersburg PA
CBHW050734230626
47052CB00002BA/183